She wasn'

If finding Reuben Page's killer meant finding a way to deal with Seth Cartwright, then she'd swallow her pride and frustration—and ignore that little frisson of nervous awareness that made her heart beat faster.

"I am looking for a story. I'm writing an article on the history of—"

"I don't care if you're writing haiku." Seth settled back behind the wheel, but his heat and scent—and mistrust—remained. "I don't need you asking questions and stirring up trouble at the Riverboat."

"Afraid I'm a security risk you can't handle?"

His eyes darkened. "I can handle *you* just fine, Miss Page."

JULIE MILLER

UP AGAINST THE WALL

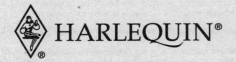

HARLEQUIN®

TORONTO • NEW YORK • LONDON
AMSTERDAM • PARIS • SYDNEY • HAMBURG
STOCKHOLM • ATHENS • TOKYO • MILAN • MADRID
PRAGUE • WARSAW • BUDAPEST • AUCKLAND

This one is for me.
Because some years are harder than others.

ISBN-13: 978-0-373-69276-7
ISBN-10:   0-373-69276-5

UP AGAINST THE WALL

ABOUT THE AUTHOR

Julie Miller attributes her passion for writing romance to shyness and all those fairy tales she read growing up. Encouragement from her family to write down all those feelings she couldn't express became a love for the written word. She gets continued support from her fellow members of the Prairieland Romance Writers, where she serves as the resident "grammar goddess." This award-winning author and teacher has published several paranormal romances. Inspired by the likes of Agatha Christie and Encyclopedia Brown, Ms. Miller believes the only thing better than a good mystery is a good romance.

Born and raised in Missouri, she now lives in Nebraska with her husband, son and smiling guard dog, Maxie. Write to Julie at P.O. Box 5162, Grand Island, NE 68802-5162.

Books by Julie Miller

HARLEQUIN INTRIGUE
719—KANSAS CITY'S BRAVEST*
748—UNSANCTIONED MEMORIES*
779—LAST MAN STANDING*
819—PARTNER-PROTECTOR**
841—POLICE BUSINESS**
880—FORBIDDEN CAPTOR
898—SEARCH AND SEIZURE**
947—BABY JANE DOE**
966—BEAST IN THE TOWER
1009—UP AGAINST THE WALL†

*The Taylor Clan
**The Precinct
†The Precinct: Vice Squad

CAST OF CHARACTERS

Seth Cartwright—KCPD vice squad detective on a dangerous undercover assignment. Hard to take down in a fight. Harder to crack his cynical heart.

Rebecca Page—She has no love for the KCPD or the gung-ho cops of the Cartwright clan who have gotten in the way of her reporting a story more than once. But no one will stop her from uncovering the truth about her father's murder.

Teddy Wolfe—Major owner of the Riverboat Casino. Suave, sophisticated and deadly. His eye for the ladies is matched only by his penchant for violence.

Shaw McDonough—Teddy's right-hand man.

Austin Cartwright—Seth's father has an addiction that can destroy anyone who cares about him.

Sarah Cartwright—Seth's twin sister. She has picked a really bad time to take a walk on the wild side.

Cooper Bellamy—Seth's partner. His job is to ghost Seth and provide a link to KCPD and the outside world.

Reuben Page—Rebecca's father. What secrets did this legendary journalist uncover? And who murdered him to kill the story?

Prologue

Three years ago

Reuben Page knelt over the bloody corpse of his informant and cursed. "Damn, Dani."

His stomach soured. Maybe he was getting too old for this type of investigative reporting. The kid had just started her Master's degree. Couldn't be more than a year or two older than Reuben's own daughter. Danielle Ballard was still a government intern, filing papers for Kansas City's economic development task force.

The symbolism of the young woman's throat being slashed wasn't lost on Reuben.

Keep her from talking.

Nor was the fact that he was alone near the rundown docks on the Missouri River just north of Kansas City's City Market, long after midnight, hovering over a dead body. If Dani had been made, most likely Reuben's investigation had, too.

"Sorry, kiddo. Has to be done." Disturbing a crime scene went against years of training as a crime reporter, but Reuben needed the disk that Dani had promised to deliver tonight. It held names, numbers, bank accounts. Clear evidence of bribes. Enough information to turn Reuben's suspicions into facts.

He bit down on his conscience and leaned over the body.

Even though Dani didn't smoke, the scent of fine tobacco clung to her clothes, mixing with the salty, dank smells of blood and flesh. The night was dull, the autumn air chilled by a heavy dampness in the air that wasn't quite rain. The wash of the river was a lonely sound as it swept past in the darkness beneath the empty docks. He should be calling the cops. Calling Dani's family. Putting a blanket over her.

Instead, Reuben turned out Dani's pockets and discovered he wasn't the first to search the corpse that night. Even her raincoat had been ripped open—with the same bloody knife that had slashed her throat, judging by the dampness of the dark red traces at the seams. The only item on her was a ring of keys in her fist. Her open purse lay in a puddle beside her. Either the disk had been taken by the killer, or Dani never had it in the first place.

But on the phone that morning, Dani had sworn that she'd found evidence to prove a new breed of organized crime had come to Kansas City. Reuben had already pieced together a pattern—a rise in intimidation crimes, suspect investments that mimicked the money laundering schemes he'd written about on the police beat in Chicago, select, ruthless murders like this one. Dani's insider evidence would connect the dots, and Reuben could expose the problem and win a second Pulitzer in the process.

"It has to be here," he muttered. If the killer had it, then Reuben's story was dead.

If the killer had the disk, then so was he.

His heart beat faster and Reuben hurried his search, silently apologizing as he ran his fingers over the body, nudging it from one side to the other with the same speed and determination with which he typed out his columns on the keyboard.

When he saw the bulge in Dani's purse, he turned it inside out and dumped the contents at his feet. Though it wasn't the right shape for a disk, he might find a note, or a clue to lead him to the disk's location. "Tell me you were a smart kid." Reuben froze. "What the hell?"

Money. Not just a couple of twenties, but hundreds, no... Reuben caught the bills before the misted breeze off the river blew them away. "There has to be ten thousand dollars here." A plant. Had to be. Idealistic kids fresh out of college didn't carry that kind of cash. "What's this?"

Reuben held the tiny plastic bag up to the dim circle of light hanging over the rusted door of the warehouse behind him. He recognized the crack from his research into numerous drug-related crimes.

"A setup." One look at her dewy skin and straight white teeth, and anyone who knew the signs could tell Dani didn't use. A crusader like her wouldn't sell, either. So why...?

Reuben peered over his shoulder into the night, trusting his reporter's nose. He was being watched. But by human eyes? Or by whatever was scurrying beneath the trash bin beside him?

He breathed a measured sigh of relief when a rat darted past and disappeared through a hole in the building's foundation. But it was warning enough for him to get his butt into gear and get out of there.

Reuben pushed to his feet, pocketing the cash, the drugs and the keys. The kid was a hero in Reuben's book, and would earn a deserving mention in his next *Kansas City Journal* column. He wouldn't let the thug who'd silenced her tarnish her reputation.

Reuben's crepe-soled shoes squeaked on the damp pavement as he hurried toward the vintage Cadillac he'd parked on the street side of the warehouse. He emptied the drugs into the river, dropped the plastic bag into a trash bin, and stuffed the wad of cash into his jacket pocket. Then he sped away into the heart of downtown K.C., planning to dump the money in a foreign location where it wouldn't be traced back to Dani Ballard. Maybe he'd donate it to a shelter, or leave it in a church's mailbox. Maybe he'd head on south of the city and toss it into one of the landfills.

Reuben Page did none of those things.

One of the keys in the passenger seat winked at him as he passed beneath a street lamp. The game was still on. "Brilliant, kiddo."

The rush of discovery fueled the story composing itself inside his head as Reuben swung the car toward the city bus terminal. He reached for the key to a bus-station storage locker and tucked it into his pocket. In the same motion, he retrieved a pen and notepad, turned to a fresh page and jotted a cryptic note.

Balancing the pad on his knee and writing as he

drove couldn't make his handwriting any worse. There was only one person left in the world who could decipher his illegible scrawl, one person who looked forward to reading his notes, one person he loved and trusted enough to share them with.

Dear Rebecca, he began.

Since his wife's death a decade earlier, Reuben had started sending his story notes to his daughter. Once upon a time, his wife had translated them and typed them up for him. But now that Rebecca was away at the University of Missouri's journalism school in Columbia, following in his footsteps as a reporter, she seemed to enjoy reading them as though she was keeping up with a journal of his activities. He supposed they replaced the letters he always intended to write, but never could quite get onto paper or into an e-mail. His scribbles connected them in a way that the dangers and demands of his job rarely allowed them to. Besides, with the number of computers he'd sent to their makers, it never hurt to have a backup copy of his current work in someone else's hands.

As he sped through the fog-shrouded streets, Reuben briefly detailed Dani's murder, skipping the more graphic elements. He wrote about the disk, listed abbreviations of the names he thought would be linked to the murder. He sent his love and promised to visit Mizzou for homecoming in a couple of weeks. He pulled an envelope from his briefcase, tucked the notepad inside and addressed the package. He stuck a wad of stamps onto one corner and dropped it into a mailbox en route.

The bus terminal was a surprising hive of activity at one in the morning. Parked cars lined the street and Reuben had to squeeze his long sedan into a tiny space nearly a block away. The street lamps barely cut a path through the fog, but still he looked—peering up and down the sidewalk as he turned up his collar and checked for familiar cars. Then, when he felt certain enough that nothing beyond leaving the scene of a murder was out of the ordinary for the night, he crossed the street. Two buses were loading and unloading passengers beneath the driveway canopy on the west side of the building, and he jogged up to lose himself in the parade of travelers entering the terminal.

Inside, Reuben separated himself from the crowd and made a beeline across the lobby to the rows of storage lockers. He found number 280 easily enough and inserted the key.

The square, squat locker could have held an entire computer, but there was only one small item inside. A padded envelope with his name on it. Hunching over the open doorway to hide his prize, he slipped the disk inside his jacket. He couldn't resist a satisfied smile. "You're gonna be more famous than Deep Throat, kiddo."

When he closed the door and saw the man in the tailored suit at the coffee counter, cradling a plastic cup between his well-manicured hands, Reuben's temporary rush of victory chilled in his veins. Dani had never stood a chance. That smug son of a bitch. Publicly claiming to be a friend of the press. A friend to Kansas City. A friend to all.

The eyes that met Reuben's gaze said he was no man's friend but his own.

And the evidence to prove it was burning a hole inside Reuben's pocket.

His story wouldn't get written. Not tonight. Not by him. Maybe not ever.

Then he became aware of the bruiser with a mustache standing at the exit, watching him without blinking. Another overbuilt guard dog waited with the passengers lining up for St. Louis. Obliquely, Reuben wondered which one of them had Dani Ballard's blood on his hands. Maybe they both did. Their boss, still sipping his coffee, certainly wouldn't dirty his hands that way.

Reuben cursed beneath his breath and slowly walked toward the heart of the lobby. How had he been followed? When had he missed the car that must have been waiting for him to leave the docks? Or had they tailed him some other way? A tracking chip, maybe? He swallowed hard and gathered his thoughts. Whys and hows no longer mattered.

Justice did.

Survival seemed a mighty distant second.

He could be bold and approach the man at the counter, disk in hand, and dare him to deny the truth. Or he could take a chance.

The same chance Danielle Ballard had taken.

With a firm resolution, Reuben Page pulled his shoulders back and exhaled a steadying breath. With his gaze darting from one threat to the next, he strode with purpose to the center of the crowded waiting area.

And tossed the ten grand of cash into the air.

As the passengers converged and chaos erupted, Reuben shoved his way past them and ran. Once-weary citizens attacked the free money with a frenzy that blocked the two thugs and gave Reuben a clear path to the door. He shot outside, never sparing a glance behind him until he reached his car.

There was no finesse to slamming the bumper of the car in front of him, no apology for scratching a strip of paint from headlamp to taillight. He jerked the wheel, floored the accelerator and sped into the street. He turned two corners and ran one stop sign before daring to turn on his lights. Hopefully, he'd gotten enough of a lead that the three men couldn't follow him.

No such luck.

Now he was painfully aware of the screech of tires and blare of horns behind him as the men who wanted to silence him closed the gap between them. Though little more than a pair of lights in the fog behind him, they closed in with an ominous intent. His own low-slung Caddy bottomed out over a pothole as he barreled through town. The base of skyscrapers gave way to empty parks, then tiny homes. The sleek black car chasing him took shape and color as it rammed his rear bumper. He skidded on the pavement made slick by the drippy fog and careened into a narrow alley. A gunshot cracked his rear window and a telephone pole tore off his side mirror as he whipped past.

Reuben couldn't remember breathing, much less turning toward the decaying isolation of the warehouses that lined the river. Another gunshot shattered the rear window and debris slammed into the back of his neck and scalp. The lacerations burned, startled. The steering wheel lurched in his grip.

He thought of his daughter as the sedan flew off the end of the dock and plunged into the river. The water was a cold shock that slapped him in the face and sharpened his senses. The heavy car sank quickly, but as the murky water pooled around him, Reuben had the presence of mind to unhook his seat belt and swim up through the empty rear window.

He kicked to the surface as the current carried him downstream. Reuben coughed up water and gasped for breath. But bright car lights from the street that ran the length of the docks caught him in their glare. Shouts and bullets followed, and he dove beneath the water again.

Rebecca would love an adventure like this one. She'd inherited her mother's beauty, but she had his tenacity. His reckless determination to know.

Reuben slammed into the rusting steel hull of the abandoned *Commodore* riverboat, permanently anchored and left to be sold for scrap metal. As his breath whooshed from his chest and he sank beneath the water, Reuben thought like a father, not a reporter. He didn't want Rebecca risking her life for a news story. He didn't want her to wind up like Dani Ballard.

As he swallowed a lungful of dense green-brown water, he wished his daughter could content herself with marrying a nice young man and filling a sweet suburban home with babies. Reuben knew Rebecca would love her children just as fiercely as he loved her. Maybe he should have showed her better what was in his heart.

The chance to meet those grandchildren, the chance to tell Rebecca the things he should have told her long ago, gave Reuben the strength to kick to the surface one last time. He hoisted himself up over the edge of the boat and rolled onto the deck. Sapped of strength, he crawled to the nearest opening and tumbled between the rotting floorboards, crashing down to the lower deck.

Shaking his vision clear, he staggered to his feet. The grandeur of what had once been a row of staterooms was lost on him. He saw only two-by-fours and steel joists and a rickety ladder descending into the pit of the engine room. Hearing footsteps running along the dock, he slid down into the bowels of the ship. Reuben slipped the disk from his pocket and hid the envelope inside the first cubbyhole he could find. Then, limping to the nearest exit, he pulled a marker from his pocket and scribbled a crude code of symbols on his hand in a shorthand that only Rebecca would understand.

"Mightier than the sword," he rasped. He hoped. He prayed.

Reuben was lightheaded and weak when muscular arms pulled him back to the *Commodore*'s deck and propped him up against the bulkhead.

"Well, if it isn't the legendary Reuben Page. You wouldn't be planning another exposé now, would you? Where's the disk Dani gave you?"

"I don't know what you're talking about."

The voice laughed without amusement. "I'm afraid the truth is going to die with you, Mr. Page."

Reuben blinked the face and suit into focus and stood as tall as his battered body would let him. "The truth never dies."

"It does tonight."

Chapter One

"W.I." Rebecca Page read the acronym out loud. "That has to be Wolfe International."

She gently turned the tattered page and read the names and information enclosed there.

TW,Sr/TW,Jr/DK/AC

Don't worry. Will dec. gibberish at earl.con. unless you get it done first.

DB dead. Removed plant. Kid clean.

Execution confirms suspicions. KCPD will need different kind of proof, however.

Pursue lead to bus locker. DB promised disk. Should name names. Someone on Econ Dev Comm in it up to his eyeballs. Influence certain. Too much money floating around KC. It's here at the docks. My nose can smell a rat—and he's a big one. They're watching me, so I know I'm onto something.

Stay away from this one, kiddo. Just play bookkeeper for me.

Will copy you as soon as able. See you at
Mizzou.
    XXOO,
    Dad

"Love you, too." Rebecca turned to the back of the
small notebook and looked at the boxes and letters
she'd copied herself. It was the last cryptic message her
father had left for her. DBD->COM. <u>AF A1/2 AS</u> .
Over the last several months, she'd added a spiderweb
of names and possible interpretations. "What were
you trying to tell me, Dad?"

As always, the answer toyed with her thoughts but
escaped her.

She tenderly closed the notebook and lifted it to her
nose, inhaling deeply. If she closed her eyes and
imagined hard enough, she could still detect her
father's familiar scent on the soft, well-worn leather.
She could hear his throaty laugh and feel his arms
wrapping her up in a warm hug.

But she was long past sitting on the sidelines and
playing bookkeeper. Rebecca wasn't a woman given
to fanciful notions, nor did she waste her time when
there was a story to pursue. She had big footsteps to
fill as a reporter for the *Kansas City Journal*. This
wasn't just about living up to her father's reputation
and making a name for herself in her chosen career.
This was about living up to her father's love. This was
about proving his faith in her hadn't been misplaced.

Her artificially long lashes tickled her cheeks as
she opened her eyes and steeled herself for the task at
hand. The only thing that warmed her tonight was the

muggy summer heat. The only scents were the faint, seaweedy smell of the Missouri River and her own spicier perfume. The only laughter she heard belonged to a few of the lucky customers outside the Riverboat Casino complex, waiting for a cab or valet service. The players who'd been less fortunate filled the night air with damning curses and desperate ramblings.

Rebecca watched them all from the front seat of her cherry-red Mustang. Was *he* the one? Was *she?*

Who were the big guns with money-laundering and murder on their minds? And who were the innocent bystanders, unaware of the big money, big influence and big cover-up hidden beneath the Riverboat Casino's polished-steel facade and glitzy excitement? They'd all come to the shiny steamship that had once been the rusted wreck of the *Commodore* riverboat. Renovation and expansion could only mask the *Commodore*'s secrets. A new name and facelift didn't change the fact that her father's life had ended here.

And where the trail of clues he'd left for her ended, her investigation would begin. If she could unlock the details of that last exposé her father had been working on, she just might be able to piece together the rest of the puzzle and find out who'd murdered him. Which was a hell of a lot more than those pathetic all-talk, no-action bozos at KCPD had been able to do over the past three years. They'd relegated Reuben Page's murder to their unsolved cold-case files.

Rebecca had no intention of giving up on her father. His memory was all she had left.

With her nerve firmly set into place, Rebecca locked the precious notebook inside the glove compartment and inhaled a deep, fortifying breath. Squeezing the university class ring that hung from a white-gold chain around her neck, she whispered, "This one's for you, Dad."

She bussed the man-sized ring with a quick kiss and tucked it inside the décolletage of her little black dress. Once out of the car, she paused for a moment to adjust the swingy hemline that stopped several inches above her knees. Any day of the week she preferred the practicality of jeans and khakis over a dress and three-inch heels. But what was the point of standing five-foot-ten if a girl couldn't show off a little leg when the occasion called for it?

Tonight's game plan definitely called for it.

As did the free fall of curly brunette hair that tickled the bare skin between her shoulder blades. Rebecca paused to open her tiny purse and pull out her compact, ostensibly to check the subtle pout of her ruby-tinted lips. In reality, she was verifying that the miniature recorder she carried would be ready at the push of a button should she need it. Tonight was more about identifying the players she'd been researching rather than finding any meaningful facts. If she could ingratiate herself into the casino crowd, get the layout of the place and the faces memorized, then she'd be in position to start digging beneath the surface. Deck by deck. Suspect by suspect. Clue by clue.

The *Journal* hadn't sanctioned this assignment. Her editor had no idea of the personal nature of this investigation. He probably wouldn't have granted her vacation if he'd known what she was really up to. But blessing or no, she intended to approach this job with the same diligence she'd use on any other story she was reporting. She intended to be just as prepared, just as thorough.

Rebecca snapped her bag shut and let the masquerade begin.

She curved her mouth into a subtle pout at the appreciative glances and outright stares that followed her across the wide, fixed gangplank leading over the water to the Riverboat's light-studded entryway. Good. She didn't have the money to throw around at the gaming tables necessary to garner the attention of the men she was here to investigate. And she couldn't exactly flash her press pass or use her real name, in case someone connected her to her father or the paper.

But there was more than one way to get herself invited into the back rooms and private offices on board. And though it stuck in her feminist craw, Rebecca Page was relying on the long legs she'd inherited from her father and the dramatic sculpt of cheekbones she'd inherited from her mother to get her inside that inner circle to the secrets hidden there.

The noise of bells and whistles, chatter and music assaulting her ears nearly sent Rebecca back out the sliding glass doors. But, seeing the wine-red carpet and refined appointments of an Old South cruise ship as some sort of surreal memorial to her father, she curled her toes inside her stilettos and refused to retreat. Bright lights and false fronts aside, this was where her father had died. It was where he might have hidden a disk or notebook before taking a bullet and plunging into the river.

His killer worked here. Or played here. Had rebuilt

the place from below the waterline on up to the bright-red smokestacks. Someone here knew something or somebody. The money that had created this gambling mecca was tainted. Her father had known that and had been silenced for that knowledge.

If she couldn't find the actual killer, then Rebecca was certain this place would provide the clues to lead her to him.

"Welcome to the Riverboat." A young woman wearing a mini version of a dance-hall girl's costume pressed a brass coin into Rebecca's hand. "We're giving a token to every new player who comes in tonight. It's good for one game at the quarter slots, or a free drink at the Cotton Blossom bar."

Rebecca glanced at the token in her palm, arching an eyebrow with skepticism. "How do you know I'm a new player? You've been open since the Memorial Day weekend, haven't you? Maybe I've been in here before."

The hostess's blank expression told Rebecca she'd interrupted the girl's memorized spiel. Then the young woman laughed.

"Okay." Rebecca waited for a "like, totally" to pop out of the blonde's giggly mouth. "So we're really giving a token to every customer who comes through our doors all summer long, whether it's your first time or not. We want you to play the games and feel at home."

In the enemy's camp? Not likely. Rebecca returned a smile to the two men who entered behind her and who walked past before she dropped the token into her

purse. Her questions had only just begun. She scanned
the bubbly golden girl's nametag. "Who's 'we', Dawn?
You and the other dance-hall girls?"

"Of course, us. Oh, you mean, who's in charge?"

Rebecca nodded, gesturing around her and acting
duly impressed. "Somebody laid out a pretty penny for
this extravaganza."

She knew the names on public record, but it
wouldn't hurt to know who the employees felt they
really had to answer to. And if the perky blonde was
willing to chat…

Dawn greeted two more guests and handed out
tokens before she answered. "Well, there's Mr.
Kelleher. He does a lot of the boring business stuff."

Rebecca ticked the name off her memorized list.
That would be the chief financial backer from the
Kansas City area. Local gossip claimed he had a
grudge against the Westin family, who owned another
wildly successful casino about two miles farther down
river. Just how far would Kelleher go to get one up on
the Westins? Would he murder a man whose story
could close him down before he ever opened for
business?

The hostess greeted another guest and continued,
enjoying the opportunity to show off her inside knowledge of the place. "Let's see. There's the security guy.
He used to be a bouncer, but now he's in charge. Never
smiles. And I don't know Mr. Cartwright's title, but I
guess he designed the place and now he's, you know,
like the fix-it-up guy? Except he doesn't do the work
himself. I see him here more than I do Mr. Kelleher."

Cartwright? Rebecca's blood simmered as her

subtle interrogation took a sharp turn into unexpected personal territory. That was a name she could have lived without hearing again. Shauna Cartwright was the stubborn lady commissioner of the KCPD whom Rebecca had interviewed more than once since assuming the position of crime beat reporter for the *Journal*. Even though the older woman had ultimately earned Rebecca's grudging respect, she couldn't exactly say they were friends. And, as if the chief cop wasn't difficult enough to get along with, an even bigger thorn in Rebecca's side was the commissioner's bull-headed son, Seth Cartwright.

Another cop.

Built like a tank. To compensate for height issues, no doubt. Rebecca might even be a shade taller than KCPD's lean, mean, testosterone machine.

But there was no debating the vivid memory of taut, hard muscles. Once, they'd been pressed intimately against her, and all that man and heat had left an indelible imprint on her skin and her psyche. Contact with Seth Cartwright had ignited her temper, along with something at the core of her that made so little sense that she'd dismissed it. Denied it, actually.

Maybe if her previous run-ins with the detective had had more to do with passion, and less to do with her right and his refusal to get to the heart of a story, she wouldn't resent this visceral response to the mere mention of his name.

The prickly sea of goose bumps bathing her skin was no trick of the Riverboat's air conditioning. Rather, it was an involuntary response to the humiliating memory of being wrestled to the ground like a common criminal. Like an overprotective bulldog, Cartwright had pinned her beneath him to keep her from approaching his mother and questioning her about a baby's murder that had sent the entire city into a panic nearly eight months ago. The jerk. Hadn't he ever heard of freedom of the press? Or respect for a woman? Or…hell.

Rebecca rubbed her arms to dispel the unwanted memory that refused to fade from her body. The name had to be a coincidence and she was doing a mental freak for no reason. A cop in his mid-twenties couldn't have put away enough money to invest in an operation like this one.

Unless he'd quit the force and gotten a new job. Or was on the take.

Now *there* was a story she'd love to sink her teeth into.

"And there's Teddy, of course."

Rebecca dragged her attention back to the present and Dawn's eager smile. "Teddy?"

Her father's ring burned against her skin inside her dress. Rebecca fisted her hand around her purse to keep from reaching for it. How could she have forgotten her purpose here, even for a moment? How had she let a man, especially *that* one, distract her from her investigation?

Burying all thoughts of her nemesis at KCPD, Rebecca asked, "Who's Teddy?"

"I mean, *Mister* Wolfe, of course," Dawn's cheeks pinkened as she corrected herself. "He manages the casino, bars and restaurants. He's more of a people person than Mr. Kelleher."

Now the name registered. Theodore Wolfe, Jr. Daniel Kelleher's not-so-silent partner. Rebecca's colleague in charge of the *Journal*'s business pages said Wolfe was a British investor who'd come to the U.S. to expand the successful gaming establishments his father's company owned in London, Monte Carlo and the Bahamas—Wolfe International. Did his arrival in Kansas City have anything to do with her father's death?

But Dawn was still talking. No, *gushing* was a better word. "You should get a load of that British accent. If James Bond had a twin… You know, they're not all stuffy and tea and crumpets over there. At least, Teddy isn't. Now his executive assistant, on the other hand—"

"Dawn, dear—are you monopolizing this beautiful lady?"

Rebecca "got a load" of that melodic, articulate British accent an instant before the scent of fine tobacco filled the air and a hand brushed the small of her back. She stiffened at the unexpected touch, then forced herself to relax as one of the men she'd come to investigate circled around her. Theodore Wolfe, Jr. Thirty. Boy wonder of the business world. As handsome in person as his publicity photo had indicated. Rebecca tipped her chin, unaccustomed to meeting many men she had to look up to. Teddy had expensive taste in smokes, deep-blue eyes and a killer smile that could make a woman with twice Dawn's experience blush like a schoolgirl.

He also had a thick-necked sidekick who positioned himself behind his shoulder. Rebecca was guessing the older man with the nearly-shaved, silver hair was the executive assistant Dawn had sneered about. Looking more bodyguard than business associate, despite his tailored suit and tie, he stood far enough away to be removed from the conversation, but close enough for Rebecca to see his dark eyes studying her, then dismissing her as though she wasn't worth his interest.

Cold, Rebecca thought, looking away before another attack of goose bumps betrayed her. *Creepy.*

"The idea is for you to welcome each guest," Teddy chastised and flirted at the same time, though Rebecca wasn't sure if the charm was aimed at her or Dawn. "Then we send them on his or her way to enjoy their evening. We want them to play."

"We were just chatting, *Mister Wolfe,*" Dawn emphasized, as though she'd earn points for making the distinction.

With his silent shadow glowering just a few feet away, it wasn't as difficult as Rebecca would have liked to respond to Teddy Wolfe's smile. "I hope I didn't get Dawn into trouble," she apologized. "She really has been very welcoming."

"She's a good girl, isn't she?" Though Dawn beamed at the praise, Rebecca thought she detected a subtle slur in the word *girl*. As opposed to *woman*. As opposed to the heavy-lidded interest he gave to Rebecca's long legs and the deep plunge of her neckline.

Score one for the femme fatale persona she'd donned for the evening. Rebecca forced herself to breathe normally, despite the surge of confidence racing through her veins. This guy was interested. If she played her cards right, and didn't come on too strong with a barrage of questions, he'd eventually tell her everything she wanted to know about his new business, and whether any blood—namely, her father's—had been spilled to make it happen.

Rebecca's sultry, satisfied smile drew his gaze up to her mouth. "I'm Teddy Wolfe. My assistant, Shaw McDonough." He waved in the general direction of the dark-eyed hulk behind him, but never took his eyes off Rebecca. "What have you two been chatting about? Something fascinating, I expect."

"I'm Rebecca." Rebecca extended her hand before the hostess mentioned the questions she'd been asking. "This is my first time at the Riverboat, and Dawn was very graciously giving me the rundown so I wouldn't get lost."

Teddy's gaze made a reluctant descent back down to her outstretched hand. But instead of the business-like shake she was expecting, he pulled her fingers to his lips and kissed them. His grip was gentle, his lips moist and warm and as precise as that swoon-worthy accent. He'd done this before. More than once. "I'd be delighted to give you the grand tour myself. I'll even show you the private gaming rooms and offices upstairs."

Dawn's gasp was audible. "Teddy." The blonde made no effort to correct her familiar address this time. "I get off in an hour. You promised…"

And though Rebecca saw the accusatory look on the young girl's face, Theodore Wolfe, Jr., ignored it.

Maybe there was something more than a crush on

the handsome Brit that Rebecca had intruded upon here. Or maybe it was the sudden wedge of Shaw McDonough between boss and hostess that soured Dawn's expression.

McDonough whispered into his employer's ear. Another British accent, though deeper, gruffer. "Daniel Kelleher is waiting in your office, Mr. Wolfe. He wants to review the agenda for the meeting regarding the poker tournament coming up next weekend."

"Of course he does." Teddy leaned in to Rebecca as though he was sharing some inside joke. "I expect Kelleher plans an agenda for each trip to the loo. If he wasn't so damn good with numbers, he'd annoy me." The smooth stroke of his thumb across the back of her knuckles reminded Rebecca that he still held her hand. "I've enjoyed meeting you. Rebecca."

She ignored the urge to pull away and reach for Dawn. A reassuring hug was definitely not a femme fatale move. Instead, she fixed her pout into place. "Maybe if I haven't lost all my money and I'm still here later, I'll take you up on that private tour."

His grip tightened as he stroked her hand again. "Be here."

"Mr. Wolfe." His executive assistant tapped his watch. "The meeting?"

"Dawn." Teddy draped his arms around the hostess's shoulders and kissed her cheek, despite her stiff posture. "Now, now. Give Rebecca all the tokens she can carry. I want her evening here to be long and successful."

"Sure, Teddy."

For a moment, she had the boss's full attention. "What was that?"

"Yes, sir, *Mister Wolfe.*"

He traced his finger across her cheek. "Ahh. Where's that pretty smile?" His wink restored Dawn's color, and a playful jab at her chin earned a soft giggle. "Good girl."

"We still need to talk. Remember?"

Teddy Wolfe turned away without an answer. He took center stage, striding through the maze of slot machines that filled the main room, shaking hands and greeting players as he passed. Shaw McDonough, with his ever-watchful scowl, scanned the crowd, urging his employer forward whenever a conversation lasted more than a few seconds.

Once the two Brits reached the boat's grand staircase at the far end of the room and headed up the stairs, Dawn turned and shoved her entire cup of tokens into Rebecca's hands. The smile she'd given the boss was gone. "Here. Enjoy your evening at the Riverboat. All of it."

Rebecca cringed at the accusation in the younger woman's voice. She wondered if there were any words she could put together to get back into Dawn's good graces without giving away her real purpose here. But guilt chased away her normal fluency, and all she could come up with was, "Thank you."

Dawn didn't even want to hear that much from her. Just as well. Rebecca was here to dig up a story, not make friends.

She had that scenario down to an art form.

She bristled at the silent admission, then straightened as if Dawn's cold shoulder didn't bother her one damn bit. "Can you point me toward the nearest Cosmopolitan?"

In reality, she'd be drinking ginger ale. But a bar tended to be a friendly place where people were either too drunk or too eager to please, making it easy to get them to talk.

With a roll of her eyes, Dawn pointed to the Cotton Blossom, a brightly lit archway which nearly blinded Rebecca to the dark woods and brass trim inside. "Knock yourself out."

Then Dawn announced to the other hostesses at the bank of doors that she was taking a break. Ignoring their reminders that each of them had already had their fifteen, she wove her way along the same path Teddy Wolfe had taken. Though, instead of following him up the stairs, she paused at the curving white balustrade. The feathers on her headpiece stirred as she tilted her chin in some mark of pride or defiance.

She glared back over her shoulder, making sure Rebecca understood that her welcome to the Riverboat had only been superficial. Teddy Wolfe was off limits— whether her intentions were personal or professional.

Then, with a stamp of her button-top boots, the blonde turned and disappeared through a shadowed recess beneath the staircase, letting the door marked Employees Only swing shut behind her.

Chapter Two

Left to fend for herself, Rebecca spent an hour strolling around the islands of slot machines and gaming tables, pausing to watch a craps game before trying her hand at blackjack.

She hadn't been entirely alone. Two men had offered to buy her a drink. Another coaxed her to rub his cards for luck. And when the dealer turned over a card and gave him 21, he invited her to be his good-luck charm at the Riverboat's upcoming high-stakes poker tournament. Rebecca agreed to think about it. Serving as arm candy was one way to get into the Riverboat's inner circle. But it wouldn't give her much of a chance to talk without drawing undue attention to her questions. Still, she took the man's card. If she couldn't create her own access into Wolfe International's secrets, then she'd show up as retired businessman Douglas Dupree's date.

"Congratulations again, miss." There was a smattering of applause from the guests lined up behind Rebecca as the dealer pushed another stack of chips her way.

Good grief. She must be up to over four hundred dollars by now—and that didn't even count the tokens Dawn had shoved into her hands earlier.

"Thanks." She added her chips to the cup of tokens, catching the ones that spilled over in her hand. She looked across at the young man wearing the Riverboat's ubiquitous uniform of a silk vest and pinstriped shirt with black armbands and string tie. "Is it bad form if I walk away from the table while I'm ahead?"

The dealer grinned. "Around here, we call that good sense." He scooped up the cards and the chip she left him as a tip. "Enjoy the rest of your evening."

Two guests vied for her lucky seat as she got up. Pushed aside for the moment, she searched for her next information target.

Despite her amazing success, Rebecca was bored with the tables. And after already sounding out the dealers on some of the same questions she'd asked Dawn Kingsley, she'd run out of connections to explore here. Though she hadn't wasted her time, there were faster, more direct ways to get the results she wanted. She needed to get chummy with an employee farther up the hierarchy—if not Teddy Wolfe, his partners and executive staff themselves.

Besides, she sensed she was drawing someone's attention. And not in the way she'd intended. The feeling of being watched was too intense, too malevolent to attribute to the legs or the hair or the little black dress. Was it the pit boss with the long black ponytail, who seemed to show up in her peripheral vision every time she placed a bet? Was it Dawn's jealous evil eye, condemning Rebecca for distracting the boss she'd already set her sights on? Could it be a potential mugger, sizing her up to rob her of her winnings once she left the cameras and security of the casino?

Or was there someone else she needed to guard against?

Rebecca shivered, feeling those eyes on her even now as she stood outside the entrance to the Cotton Blossom Bar.

A subtle glance to either side revealed no one more suspicious than the next person. Short of spinning around and making eye contact with every soul on the Riverboat's vast main floor, there was nothing she could do to identify and stop the unwanted interest.

Watch my back, Dad, she prayed, invoking her father's memory and finding her own strength.

Her laid-back father would have hated a place like this, with all its glitz and glam and commotion. But she could feel him with her, like a restless spirit lurking in the shadows until revelation of the truth could finally give him peace. Rebecca fingered the chain around her neck, imagining his warmth before the chill of isolation could take hold of her.

"Has to be done," she whispered. She tipped her chin, stood straight and tall, and walked into the bar.

Rebecca nodded to the faceless bouncer who waved her inside without checking her license. Her eyes needed a moment to adjust to the dimmer ambiance, her ears to the more human, less mechanical sounds. By the time she'd pulled up a stool at the polished walnut bar and ordered her ginger ale and lime, she'd introduced herself to the bartender, Tom Sawyer.

"You're kidding, right?" She looked up from the

nametag on his black silk vest and offered a teasing smile.

"My mother was an English teacher. She had a thing for literature." The dexterous giant who created drinks with a speedy sleight of hand winked and moved down the bar to fill the cocktail waitress's drink order, clearing away abandoned glasses as he went. The literary giant was too busy to press for information right now. So Rebecca pulled the straw between her lips and swiveled around to seek out other prospects.

Most of the tables were filled with gamblers celebrating their jackpots or drowning their losses. Some were doing their best to impress a date, others were hoping to find one. The lone waitress, in a short, showboat-style costume that matched Dawn's, was running like crazy to fill orders and clear tables. "Two drafts and two rum and colas, Tom."

Rebecca traded a sympathetic smile with the other woman as she brushed a droopy feather off her forehead and leaned against the brass railing to catch her breath for a moment. But the instant she rested her full weight on her left arm, the waitress winced and pulled back, drawing Rebecca's attention to the dark violet and purple marks on her wrist.

The bartender had noticed them, too. "You sure you're okay to work tonight, Melissa? I can ask Mr. Wolfe to call in someone else."

"No. Don't do that." But, realizing she may have answered too quickly, the waitress tucked her long, golden hair back into its French twist and smiled. "You know I need the tip money."

"I'll stake you for it," Tom offered. "Go home and rest that arm."

"I am not taking charity from you. Now load up my drinks." She gritted her teeth as she lifted the tray in her left hand. "But thanks."

Melissa was too busy to do Rebecca much good, either. And she didn't think any of the customers could give her the kind of information she needed. Maybe the bar would be a bust tonight. Was it too soon to go snooping through the offices and private rooms upstairs? Of course, it was. But Rebecca had been hoping to find some piece of evidence on this first visit to the Riverboat. At least a clue that would point her in the direction of something useful.

"Mr. Cartwright?"

Rebecca froze with a sip halfway up her straw as the bartender called to someone in the archway behind her. There was that name again. No. The fates wouldn't be that cruel. *C'mon, Dad. You're supposed to be watching out for me here.*

She slowly turned. Ginger ale pooled back in her glass as she breathed again. *Not* Seth Cartwright.

Though the stocky build of the man buttoning his cream-colored jacket reminded her of the burly detective, the similarities ended there. This man had enough gray on his head to give his blond hair a silver sheen. His suit and tie and easy smile were a definite contrast to the streetwise style and smart-mouth attitude of his namesake at KCPD. This distinguished fellow must be the "fix-it-up" guy Dawn had said was in charge of *something* at the casino. He was definitely an acquaintance she needed to make.

So when he sidled onto the stool beside her, and his knee brushed against hers, Rebecca returned his glance with a smile. "Hi."

The older man eyed the cup of chips and tokens sitting on the bar beside her drink. "Looks like you're having a good night."

"You know what they say—first time's lucky."

"That they do." He traced his finger around the rim of the cup. He picked up a blue and white chip, flipping it with a magician's dexterity between his fingers before placing it back on top of the pile. "What's your game? Slots? Roulette? Craps?"

This guy was definitely a player she wanted to meet. "I like card games."

"A little strategy to balance the luck, eh?" He tapped the token on top of her pile. "You know, you can trade these in for a ticket. It's easier—and safer—than carrying around tokens or chips or cash. I can show you how to exchange them."

The blackjack dealer had already told her how. "I'd appreciate that."

"I'm Austin, by the way." Unlike Teddy Wolfe, this man offered her a traditional handshake. "I'm the architect responsible for redesigning this place."

"I'm Rebecca." The bar was looking up, after all. She'd think of this potential source as Austin, and let the whole Cartwright coincidence slide. "The Riverboat is lovely. I feel like I've gone back in time with these surroundings."

"Authentic as the retro look is, everything behind the historic facade is completely high-tech. I did all the research and design elements myself." Perfect. A man who bragged about his accomplishments was a man who liked to talk. About a lot of things. Maybe she could even get him to show her the blueprints for this place. Rebecca had hit paydirt.

"So, you know the Riverboat inside and out?"

"Probably better than anybody."

"Mr. Cartwright." The bartender demanded Austin's attention again.

"You'd better take care of business," she suggested.

Pressing for information right now would only arouse suspicion. She'd follow up with Austin later. Maybe ask him to show her around. He could take her into the bowels of the boat, into the parts that would have been in place at the time of her father's death. She imagined she could learn more from that tour than from the places she suspected Teddy Wolfe wanted to show her.

"What's up, Tom?" the older man asked.

"Can you speak to Mr. Wolfe about getting another waitress for this shift? When one of them calls in sick like tonight... At least bring someone in off the gaming floor. Melissa's running ragged."

"Is she complaining?" Austin asked.

"Of course not. You know her."

Rebecca turned the direction he pointed and saw the waitress schooling her patience with a smile at a table with three college-aged men who were flirting with her. While Tom and Austin discussed options across the bar, Rebecca noted how Melissa flexed her fingers on her sore arm before collecting their empty beer bottles. She was mentally girding herself to take the extra weight. Once she had the bottles and the order, she turned back toward the bar.

But, with a suggestive quip, one of the men reached for her, tugging her off balance. Melissa yelped in pain and the tray went flying.

Rebecca was on her feet before the last beer bottle hit the floor and shattered.

The man who'd caused the accident was instantly apologetic, but Melissa waved him off when he tried to help. "No. It's fine. Really. Don't get up. Please."

Rebecca picked up two intact bottles and righted them on the tray before squatting down beside the blond waitress. "Here. Let me."

Melissa paused in her frantic retrieval of the broken brown glass. "This isn't your job." Her blue eyes were moist and wide with unshed tears as she met Rebecca's gaze. She dropped a shard onto the tray and cradled her left arm against her chest. "I can do it. I have to."

Son of a bitch.

Lifted up to the subdued light of the bar's chandeliers, the pattern of bruises on Melissa's swollen wrist became evident. Five of them. With the span of long, strong fingers. The imprint of a man's hand.

Rebecca swallowed the bile in her throat and reached for the next shard of glass. "I'm helping," she insisted, resisting the urge to ask who'd hurt her. Was it Tom? Was that why he was so protective and anxious to get her off the floor? Was it a customer? Boyfriend? Husband?

She'd written pieces on domestic violence before. She knew the numbers to call, the words to say. But her dad… She owed him so much. Could she help Melissa without betraying a plan that had been months in the making?

"I'm helping," she repeated, positioning herself between Melissa and Tom when the bartender hurried over with a towel to mop up the splatters of beer.

Maybe making a friend tonight, making *this* friend, was just as important as finding her father's killer. Maybe there was more than one story here on the Riverboat, more than one reason why Rebecca needed to become a part of this world and discover all the secrets hidden here. Maybe she could help the living as well as the dead.

The perfect opportunity lay scattered at her feet.

"Hey—Melissa, is it?" The waitress nodded, blinking away the tears she refused to shed. "I'm assuming you guys have a first aid kit here. Why don't you go wrap your wrist for some extra support, and I'll cover for you for a few minutes. Just tell me which tables are waiting on drinks and I'll deliver them. I can clear away the empties, too."

When Tom seconded the idea, Rebecca wondered if he was sincere in his concern—or eager to cover the evidence of his assault.

Melissa shrugged, clearly reluctant to showcase her injury, despite the practicality of the suggestion. "I couldn't let you do that."

Rebecca grinned, including them both in her offer. "I want to." She beat big Tom to helping Melissa to her feet and carried the tray to the bar. "I've been looking for a second job to help make ends meet."

Austin was waiting for them at the waitress's station. "Melissa, are you all right?" He shifted on his feet, burying his hands in his jacket pockets. "What happened?"

"Just an accident."

He nodded, than darted a glance at Rebecca. "Thank you."

Rebecca picked up on his uneasiness. Good Lord, was *Gramps* the man responsible for her injury? He was certainly fit enough to do some damage. "No problem. I worked my way through college waiting—" that's when she noticed a handful of her chips and tokens had disappeared from her cup "—tables." Perplexed by the discovery, she couldn't quite breathe a sigh of relief. Austin was guilty of something, if not abuse. "If you could use another waitress, I'd love to have the job."

Melissa was the first to respond to the proposition. "I don't know. Really, I'll be okay. We've been short-handed before. Right, Tom?"

The big bartender glared a response. But Melissa glanced away from the message he tried to convey. Whether concern had been rebuffed or a threat satisfied, Rebecca couldn't tell. Tom dumped the mess into the trash and grumbled, "It's not my call."

"I say give her a chance." By comparison, Austin was downright enthusiastic about getting Rebecca on the payroll. "I'd be happy to run it by Mr. Wolfe. If Tom thinks you can handle it, you'd have my full recommendation. You could take care of the paperwork later."

Rebecca went along with his friendly support, pretending she didn't hear the click of metal tokens and plastic disks knocking together in his jacket pocket. She assumed he'd have some ready excuse if she did call him on the theft. Add one more suspect to her list.

Austin the Nameless One had secrets to hide. Maybe it stopped with kleptomania. Maybe it meant there were other, darker, mysteries he could reveal to her.

"Melissa, you come with me." Now the older man was eager to leave. "I'll bandage that arm for you. You?" He winked at Rebecca. "Grab an apron and start clearing those tables."

"You got it."

Everyone she'd met thus far had been polite and accepting, if not outright friendly.

Everyone she'd met thus far was hiding something as well. Her reporter's nose was telling her as much.

She was in the right place. She was in. She was going to succeed where KCPD had failed.

Her father would be proud.

Rebecca adjusted the black apron around her waist and moved to the next table to gather glasses and take their order. She'd already discovered the bar's outside entrance, and used the opportunity of clearing the deck tables to scout out where public access ended and private balconies and service corridors began. She'd met other staff, and had identified some of the Riverboat's repeat and long-term customers.

Other than wishing she'd worn more comfortable shoes, she didn't have to worry about anything else tonight. She'd be back tomorrow. She could ask her questions and begin her search then. Chat with Teddy Wolfe. Meet Daniel Kelleher. Take Austin Cartwright up on a tour. Befriend Melissa and find a way to help her.

No one would suspect a thing.

Nothing could go wrong.

But her smug smile was short-lived.

She sensed the hostile gaze boring holes into her back. More intense, more direct than anything she'd felt before. A beat of time passed before a blunt voice from her past grated against her ears.

"What the hell are you doing in my casino?"

"YOUR CASINO?" Tawny gold eyes shot sparks at him as Seth Cartwright strode through the maze of tables.

Rebecca Page. Intrepid reporter. Dogged investigator. Wouldn't say *uncle* even if it meant saving her own skin.

Caught. Snooping where the woman damn well knew she shouldn't be.

He walked right up to her until he was close enough to absorb her scent and to communicate in a whisper.

"It's a free country, so you're welcome to throw away your money in whatever way you please." Sarcasm came far too easily to Seth these days. He'd been at this job long enough that he'd learned to ignore any flicker of guilt or regret when the verbal arrows unleashed themselves. "But when you stop playing and you start chatting up the employees and customers, it's time for you to go."

Her chin tilted up. Seth expected no less from a woman who relied on guts as much as a wickedly precise intuition when it came to tracking down a news story. Her tongue was in fine form tonight, as well. "It's a pleasure to see you, too, Detective."

"Don't call me that. Not anymore."

He said the words he loathed to hear and watched the transformation cross her face. Shock. Confusion. "You're not a cop anymore?"

When the serves-you-right smirk reached those painted lips, he reached for her. "I got a better job."

"Hey." The would-be waitress dodged his grasp and turned on the attitude. She pulled her tray in front of her like a shield and tipped her nose up with that Amazon arrogance he was all too familiar with. "Then you can't arrest me."

As though besting him by a few inches had ever made him retreat.

"Is there a reason why I should? I just want you to leave." He wrapped one hand around her arm, pried the tray from her resistant grasp and started walking.

"*You* want—?" She tugged against his grip. "You have no right—"

"I'm Chief of Security around here. I have every right."

"Chief of—? No way."

"Way." He tugged back and she stumbled beside him, bumping into his shoulder, freezing for an instant in mute surprise before regaining her balance and pushing away. She felt like any other woman, with delicate breasts that poked against his arm and back, and hair dark and soft as mink that caught in his collar and brushed his neck. But Rebecca Page wasn't like any other woman. She was trouble on stilts. He didn't need the kind of curiosity and attention she thrived on to walk into the middle of his investigation.

He'd worked too damn hard for eight long months to get to where he was at Wolfe International. He'd trashed his reputation on the force, lost the loyalty of his friends and gained the trust of his enemies. He'd lied, bent a few rules, broken a few bones. He'd learned the difference between being tough and being dead. No nosy reporter—woman or otherwise—was going to waltz her way onto the Riverboat and blow his operation.

"C'mon." He slowed his pace and altered his grip to keep her on her feet and keep her moving. "I thought you'd gotten a clue last fall when you were harassing my mother about the Baby Jane Doe murder case. I don't like report—"

"Shh!" She darted in front of him and pressed her fingers over his mouth, stopping up his words. Stopping him. What the hell? An apologetic frown creased the smooth skin on her forehead. "Don't say another word," she whispered. "I don't know what you think is going on here. I was only pitching in to help Melissa. But I'll go. Just let me get my purse."

Huh? Capitulation? Seth's gaze narrowed. Had to be a tactic. But a quick study of her fervent expression revealed no clear objective. Or motive. "Whatever."

He tossed the tray on the bar and, without releasing her, picked up her little black bag.

"That's mine."

Evading her grasping fingers and annoyed huff, Seth twisted it open and spotted the keys, comb, lipstick—and cell phone-size recorder inside. Just as he'd thought. He had Little Miss Innocent's number. Seth lifted his gaze to her gold-brown eyes. Was that a plea he read there? Or defiance?

Didn't matter. *He* was in control of this situation. He snapped the purse shut and pushed it into her hands. "Pitching in to help yourself to what?" But that wide mouth was pressed into a fine, thin line. No problem.

He could remove the tape outside, away from these witnesses, and get his own answers. "Time to go bye-bye."

He reclaimed his grip on her elbow and turned her toward the doorway and the main lobby. This time she didn't protest.

But Sawyer threw his arms up behind the bar. "Hey, you're stealing my only waitress."

Rebecca glanced over her shoulder. "I'll be back."

Seth kept moving. "No, she won't."

The click of her killer heels muffled when they reached the lobby carpeting. He never had understood how a woman could walk in those things, and suspected that hurrying at his side was a difficult task, even with those long legs. But she didn't argue his hold on her arm or his path toward the front door.

He hadn't believed it when he'd first spotted her on the monitor in his security office. He'd pegged Rebecca Page as a woman who liked to stay in control of things—not an easy thing for a gambler to do. Still, he hadn't taken any chances and had radioed Ace Longbow, the pit boss on the floor tonight, to keep an eye on her. As long as she was playing, she could stay. Seth would steer clear of her and keep his suspicions in check.

But then Ace had taken a break to handle some personal business, and by the time the big Indian had reported back in, he'd lost track of Rebecca. Seth had scrolled through nearly every camera angle on his monitors before he found her at the Cotton Blossom.

There she sat, flirting with his father at the bar. Long mahogany hair down to here, short black skirt up to there. His dad's eyeballs bugged out to…hell. The woman clearly wasn't here to gamble.

Seth had long since given up on the idea of his parents ever getting back together—and he knew his mother was far better off without Austin Cartwright. Messing with the ladies had never been his dad's problem. But he had other weaknesses that an opportunist like Rebecca Page wouldn't hesitate to exploit if it meant getting her story.

And the story brewing beneath the surface of the Riverboat was too big to allow an ambitious reporter to break it before his mission here was accomplished.

If he could still accomplish it.

Seth had been out of the office in an instant, knowing this entire undercover operation could be lost with one wrong word by that woman. He couldn't get to the bar fast enough. Couldn't risk asking his father about what they'd discussed when he'd dashed past him and Melissa in the lobby. He'd been blinded by the same surge of adrenaline he'd felt when their paths had crossed in the past. Rebecca Page had to go.

Her resistance renewed once he got her out the door. No surprise there. This time she tried to reason with him. She flipped the hem of her apron at him. "I have a job here, you know."

"Where's the rest of your uniform?"

"I just started."

He got her across the gangplank. "Then you're fired."

"You can't do that."

"Watch me. Where are you parked?" He remembered the flashy red Mustang from their last encounter when she'd had the gall to stalk his mother to her home to bug her about the Baby Jane Doe murder investigation. Sure, that case had since been solved with the help of his new stepfather, and his mother's position as acting commissioner of police had become a permanent job since they'd put the killer behind bars.

But he figured once a pest, always a pest. In another profession, he might have admired Rebecca's persistence. But it was a reporter's job to make headlines. Reveal secrets. Expose facts that could do more harm than good if they became common knowledge.

Therefore, the lady with the diehard curiosity had to go before she opened her mouth.

"Give me your keys," Seth ordered, as they approached the Mustang, moving farther away from the lights and crowd of the casino. Instincts honed by months of learning to spot trouble before it spotted him had Seth checking between and underneath the vehicles before he led her to the door of her car. He snapped his fingers when he saw she wasn't complying. "The keys."

Out of sight from the front doors and beyond the hearing of other customers, she was done pretending to cooperate. She stuck her purse out at arm's length and tried to play keep-away. "Can't you ever just ask nicely when you want something?"

The role he'd been forced to play since taking this assignment didn't involve making *nice.* People who *asked* got trampled on in this business.

So he grabbed her outstretched arm, spun her around and backed her against the car while he snatched the black bag from her grasp.

"Damn you. Give me that!" Her fingers tangled in the lapels of his jacket as she tried to push him away and retrieve her purse.

"Stop." Seth leaned in half a step closer, pinning her hips and thighs in a mockery of intimacy, warning her she couldn't win this particular battle. Her struggles stilled with a startled gasp. But if she hadn't made the sharp sound of surprise, he would have. Her lips hovered at eye-level, painted red and parted, breathing little puffs of tantalizing warmth across his cheek, reminding him how long it had been since he'd risked being with a woman. How long it had been since he'd risked feeling anything beyond the job.

The imprint of her feminine shape was an unexpected shock to his system. Blood surged through his veins and things awoke. Control and denial had sustained him for months. But here he stood, caught unawares in the middle of the night, wanting something he shouldn't—needing something too dangerous even to put a name to.

Damning that weakness inside him, Seth opened her purse and fished out the keys. While she watched in mute condemnation, he removed the tape from her recorder and dropped it in the pocket of his jacket.

"That's stealing," she accused, drawing her hands from his chest and crossing her arms between them.

He'd done worse recently. "I call it a security precaution."

A cool breeze off the river blew a long, curly tendril over her flushed cheek, but didn't do a thing to soothe the fever rising in his body. He tested his restraint by refusing to move away, by denying the urge to sweep away that lock of hair that had caught at the corner of her mouth. He denied the urge to sample that corner with his tongue to find out if she was as rich and fiery to the taste as she was to the eye.

He forced Rebecca to be the one to retreat. She obliged by leaning back against the sweet lines of the car to ease a whisper of space between them.

"You are a son of a bitch," she accused, jamming the tempting strand of hair behind one ear. The husky softness of her voice was a direct contrast to the darts targeting him from those golden eyes.

He didn't argue the point. He didn't say anything as he returned her purse and slipped the key into the lock.

"Did they boot you off the force for being a jerk?" She was determined to get the upper hand he wouldn't allow.

"It is *my* right and responsibility to escort anyone off the premises whom I deem a threat."

"A threat to what?" She snatched at his sleeve and demanded he look at her. "This is about your mother, isn't it. If she and I can share a civil conversation now, then you—"

"Leave my mother out of this." Seth could do the in-your-face thing, too. "I don't want you snooping around here."

"I wasn't—"

"You don't know how to do anything else." He opened the door and pushed her inside, instinctively taking care to protect the back of her head, just as he would load up any of the suspects he'd once pulled off the streets. "Did you tell anyone here you work for the

Journal? Or were you recording conversations illegally?"

"What? No. That tape is still blank." Seth climbed in right beside her and closed the door, forcing her to scramble over the console onto the passenger seat. "Hey. Get out!"

For a split second, her backward crab crawl exposed a smooth tanned thigh all the way up to a line of black silk panty. Sheesh. Hormones lurched in a base male response to all that bare skin and he slapped his hands around the steering wheel before he reached for something he shouldn't. Rebecca Page was the enemy here. She fired his temper, not his lust.

She threatened his mission, not his conscience.

Tender feelings like guilt or concern had no place in the world of power and intimidation in which he'd immersed himself.

And he was too smart to forget that.

He wisely averted his gaze while she hastily sat up in her seat and righted her skirt and the apron she wore. He went on the attack before he did something foolish, like ask if he'd been too rough with her. "Why are you here? What story are you working on?"

She tucked the heavy charm at the end of her necklace back inside the front of her dress. "I'm here to make friends and earn some extra money with a part-time job."

"Liar."

"Ass."

With a noisy huff, she folded her arms and stared out the windshield into the fog off the river.

Seth breathed deeply, right along with her, waiting

for a response. The carefully preserved interior of the small vintage car was tinged with the scents of leather polish and Rebecca's own spicy perfume. Frustrated with her stubborn silence, he raked his fingers through the careless spikes of his short blond hair. His focus should be back on the Riverboat and proving that Teddy Wolfe was just as deviant and dangerous as Interpol and KCPD suspected him to be. He shouldn't be sitting here, noticing the Mustang's fine details. And he damn well shouldn't be noticing anything about the car's owner.

"Well?" he prodded.

"You said you weren't a cop anymore. I don't have to talk."

Enough of this battle of wills. He needed to win this argument more than she could ever understand.

Seth fitted into Teddy Wolfe's world all too well. He released the steering wheel and leaned over the center console, bracing one hand on the dashboard and the other on the seat behind her head. "You'll talk to *me*."

Chapter Three

Whatever advantage Rebecca had over Seth Cartwright when they were standing vanished when they sat side by side. Now he loomed over her, and those massive shoulders and beefy chest filled up the tight space inside her car.

She smelled the dampness from the air outside that clung to his suit and golden hair. She heard his deep, even breathing over the alarming staccato of her own pulse in her ears.

He wore a classic suit over a tight charcoal-gray T-shirt. But no amount of tailored wool or self-restraint could completely civilize the hard edge that lined his square jaw, or temper the danger that lurked in the depths of his gray-green eyes.

It couldn't hide the black shoulder holster that peeked out from inside his jacket, either. Right next to the pocket with her confiscated tape. Okay, so she hadn't recorded anything on it yet, but still, he'd taken it from her. Just like that, he'd put her at a disadvantage. All that muscle intruding into her personal space made her rethink the shrimp-size memory she'd mistakenly had of the man. His sharp eye and suspicious mind made him more of a formidable opponent than the pesky annoyance she remembered. And the gun...? Oh, hell. She knew she'd be taking a risk by going undercover at the Riverboat. But she hadn't really *known*.

She'd expected close calls and the need to think on her feet. She'd reviewed her arsenal of fast talk and coy come-ons. She'd even been prepared for threats if her true purpose was found out. She'd made note of where the nearest exit in each room was located, and had her can of pepper spray within reach on her keychain. But she hadn't expected this palpable sense of mistrust, this antagonism, this isolation.

She hadn't expected to feel like the enemy herself.

The fuse on Seth Cartwright's temper, however, was every bit as short as she remembered, his inability to listen to reason just as frustrating. No wonder she didn't like cops. Or ex-cops. Or whatever kind of man rated a dubious title like Chief of Security at the place where her father had been murdered.

She'd been willing enough to leave the Riverboat with him to keep him from blabbing to everyone on board that she was a reporter for the *Journal*. But she had no intention of giving up on her quest.

She *wasn't* the bad guy here.

If finding Reuben Page's killer meant finding a way to deal with Seth Cartwright, then she'd swallow her pride and frustration——and ignore that little frisson of nervous awareness that made her heart beat faster. *Give me strength, Dad.* And then she asked for the practically impossible. *Give me patience.*

"You want to talk?" She bit down on a sarcastic desire to remind him how close-mouthed he'd been with her. "How about this? I *am* looking for a story."

"And?"

If he could be a smug know-it-all, then she could tell a little white lie. "I'm writing an article on the history of the *Commodore*. From its days as a cruise ship and dance-hall club on the Missouri River through its rusty demise as a floating eyesore to its reincarnation as a casino. I'm talking to owners, staff and passengers who've known the *Commodore* in all its stages, from the time it was built in the late thirties to the present."

He settled back behind the wheel. But his heat and scent—and mistrust—remained. "History? That's not your usual beat."

"I've always loved research. Between jazz and baseball and the westward expansion of our country there's so much history in Kansas City that there's always something more to learn." Those statements were completely true. The first story she'd written for her high-school paper had been a piece on the Kansas City Monarchs of the Negro Baseball League. She'd only turned to crime investigation after her father's death. "Who knows? If I can piece together enough facts and firsthand accounts, I could write a series of articles—or put together a book."

"I don't care if you're writing haiku poetry. I don't need you asking questions and stirring up trouble at the Riverboat."

"Afraid I'm a security risk you can't handle?"

His eyes darkened like storm clouds in the shadows

of the car. The bastard didn't even blink. "I can handle *you* just fine, Miss Page."

Easing any smart remark aside on a soft, drawn-out breath, she tried to keep the rare line of communication open. "You should probably call me Rebecca. I didn't tell anyone my full name tonight. I don't want them to know who I am and what I do. It could taint their responses to me." She added the latter as a plausible explanation of her need for anonymity. "It's not like I'm a television reporter with my face plastered all over the news. The *Journal* doesn't even publish a picture with my byline. I was going to use my mother's maiden name if I needed to."

He shook his head. "A decent background check would point out that deception in an instant."

"Good to know," she conceded. "Then I'll use another one. Tom Sawyer's named after a character in a book. I can come up with something at least as believable."

"You've been talking to Sawyer?"

"Just enough to get offered a job. And to make me wonder if he's the guy who got too rough with Melissa."

Seth swore. One pithy word that told her he'd noticed the abuse, too. "You *have* been a busy lady."

"I'm trained to be observant."

His answering silence lasted so long that Rebecca thought the conversation was over.

She jerked in her seat when he swung around to face her again. "If you really are concerned about Melissa, could I appeal to your kinder side?" The hard line of his mouth quirked at one corner, in something that could almost be construed as a smile. Almost. "You do have a kinder side, don't you?"

Ha. Ha. But the quiet depth of his voice kept her sarcasm in check. It stung to think his question was halfway serious. "I care very deeply about a lot of things."

He nodded, taking her statement at face value. "These aren't all nice people around here. Asking the wrong question to the wrong person could get you into trouble."

"I'm not afraid of ruffling someone's feathers."

"No need to state the obvious." He pulled her keys from his pocket and dropped them into her lap. Concession? Or dismissal? "Just know, that if you *do* ruffle somebody's feathers, I may not be there to bail you out."

"I never asked you to. I don't ask anyone for anything except the truth."

"There are some truths that could get you killed."

His stark warning filled all the empty spaces inside in the car. And, despite the warmth of the night, Rebecca felt goose bumps crawling across her skin.

But he couldn't have said anything that would make her more determined than ever to stay to find her father's killer.

"Look…Seth." Why was that word so hard to push through her lips? Had she never called him by name before? "I don't care about whatever descent into the dark side you're on. If tossing cheats and rowdy drunks out of the casino gives you the same thrill that arresting bad guys and harassing innocent reporters used to, then that's your business. I appreciate the words of caution, but you're not going to stop me from taking care of *my* business."

"You are the single most stubborn woman I have ever met. I'm trying to give you a fair—" A blast of static from beneath his coat cut him off. He reached inside and pulled a walkie-talkie from his belt. "Cartwright."

The static cleared and another man's voice reported in. "Mr. Wolfe is leaving the building to make a bank deposit. He says he'll be staying at the penthouse downtown instead of his suite on the ship tonight."

Seth checked his watch. "What about Kelleher?"

"He's staying late to work some numbers in his office."

"Post a man outside the accounting office. Tell Mr. Wolfe I'll be right there to escort the money."

Escort the money? Big money? Illegal money? What *numbers* was Daniel Kelleher working on? Probing questions danced on the end of Rebecca's tongue, but she pressed her lips together to keep them quiet. She didn't need Seth Cartwright's blessing to investigate Wolfe International and the Riverboat, but she did need him to stay out of her way and keep the whole reporter thing secret.

He hooked the phone back on his belt and adjusted his suit coat to mask his shoulders and gun. "You think you could earn Melissa's trust?"

What? He was asking *her* for a favor? But the subject was too serious for Rebecca to gloat. "I have some contacts who counsel abused women. I can call them to get ideas on the best way I…we…could help her."

"Good. You can stay. For Melissa." He pointed a

finger in warning. "But if I hear one word out of your mouth that isn't related to the history of the ship or becoming her friend, you're out of here."

Then she wouldn't let him hear anything else. Rebecca stuck out her hand. "Deal," she lied.

Maybe he sensed the false promise there. Or maybe he could hear the traitorous anticipation of his touch pounding through her veins. Seth looked down at the outstretched offering, looked up into her eyes. He looked deep enough inside her that Rebecca felt compelled to curl her fingers into her palm and cross her arms in front of her again.

"I have to go," he said. Seth dismissed her, climbed out of her car and disappeared into the night.

REBECCA SAT in the passenger seat several moments longer, hugging herself, trying to instill the warmth that victory over Seth Cartwright should have given her. She'd just negotiated her way around the biggest obstacle standing in the path of her investigation. She should be high-fiving herself, not clinging to her father's ring and wondering why the air inside her car seemed flat and cool in the wake of her charged confrontation with Seth.

Rousing herself from that disturbingly fanciful thought, Rebecca unlocked the glove compartment. She pulled out her father's notebook and turned to a new page where she jotted some notes about tonight's events and what her next step should be.

DBD—Dani Ballard Disk was her best guess for that clue.

COM—The *Commodore*. Had to be.

The wolf is at the door, her father had written on another page. "Teddy Wolfe," she mouthed out loud, underlining the name she had written. "Or someone else at Wolfe International."

"AF A1/2 AS," she read out loud. "I'll figure it out, Dad. I promise."

Rereading her father's words centered her around her purpose again, and the distractions of Seth Cartwright's scent, strength and surly attitude receded beneath a surge of renewed confidence. She'd already made an introduction to almost every major player at the Riverboat. She'd be back tomorrow night to ask more questions and poke her nose into the original parts of the ship. With luck, she could acquaint herself with Daniel Kelleher and anyone else who had stood to gain from Reuben Page's death.

With a solid plan firmly in mind, Rebecca saved herself the indignity of climbing across the front seats again and got out of the car.

"Oh, damn." As she walked around the hood to the driver's side, she realized she still wore the short black apron from the Cotton Blossom. As much as she wanted to stay off Seth Cartwright's radar screen for the rest of the night, she knew she had to venture back inside the Riverboat to return it. She could go straight to the bar and show Tom that she was serious about the job by returning the apron and asking him what time he expected her to report for work. She could avoid the main lobby altogether by circling around the outer deck to the bar's outside entrance.

But her aching feet balked at the long row of cars separating her from the Riverboat's gangplank.

"Has to be done." She coaxed her energy to return

by repeating the phrase her father had often used when she'd turned her nose up at some unpleasant task.

So Rebecca pulled off her high heels and tossed them into the car before locking it behind her. As long as she didn't step into any unidentified gooey substances, the walk actually felt good. The pavement was still warm and just rough enough to soothe her aching feet without scratching them. Tomorrow, she'd trade a little sex appeal for the comfort of more sensible shoes.

Tonight, she just wanted to assure herself of the waitressing job, maybe check on Melissa, then go home and get some sleep.

A sleek black limousine pulled up behind Rebecca as she crossed the gangplank. As the mustached chauffeur got out and circled around to open the rear passenger door, a small crowd of curious customers gathered and pointed. Rebecca idly wondered what celebrity was stopping by when she spotted Seth Cartwright having a curt conversation on his walkie-talkie, just inside the Riverboat's glass front door.

Great. Just what she needed. Another run-in with her least favorite ex-cop.

Rebecca quickly darted into the group of spectators, hoping he hadn't seen her. When Teddy Wolfe and his omnipresent shadow, Shaw McDonough, appeared in the entryway behind Seth, she breathed a little easier.

Of course. Seth wasn't guarding the door against her. That side-to-side survey of the exit area, as thorough as a hawk searching for its prey, was the Chief of Security in action—protecting the casino's assets and its owner. While they'd been hashing out a truce of sorts in her car, Seth had received a message about Teddy Wolfe's departure—along with a bank deposit that should be pretty sizable, judging by the crowd that had been here all evening.

Rebecca frowned. Wouldn't Wolfe International have a vault to store all that money? Or an armored car to transport it? Wouldn't they leave handling that much money up to security and not the man in charge?

Seth walked forward to open the sliding-glass doors, and Teddy and Shaw followed behind him. With Austin Cartwright's bragging about the high-tech underpinnings of the Riverboat, she'd certainly expected to see something more secure than the black briefcase handcuffed to Teddy's wrist.

Unless that briefcase held Teddy's personal cash.

Or something else entirely. Printouts? Contracts? Computer disks? Drugs? Counterfeit bills?

Was Teddy Wolfe in the habit of carrying evidence that could be used against him in a locked-up briefcase? Getting something like that out of the casino made sense. Keeping a low profile while doing it made even more sense.

Rebecca wanted her notepad or tape recorder. She wanted to see inside that briefcase. "What are you up to, Teddy?"

"…handsome as a movie star." The volume of the people surrounding her increased, disrupting her thoughts.

"He's a good-luck charm for his customers."

"I want to shake his hand."

"I thought we were done. You've already lost…"

"Mr. Wolfe!"

As the group she'd hidden herself among clamored

forward to greet Teddy Wolfe as though they were a bona fide fan club, Rebecca slipped into the shadows behind the deck railing away from the front door. Despite every effort from Seth and Shaw McDonough to keep Teddy moving toward the car, the casino's major partner basked in the attention of his guests. He shook hands, smiled, posed for a picture with an older woman. Kissed her cheek.

Meanwhile, Rebecca huddled against a steel strut that supported the balcony above her and watched the show play out.

Teddy, his chained-up briefcase and his adoring guests had reached the limo now. The chauffeur was patiently holding the door. Shaw McDonough stood to one side, watching the scene with an expressionless mask. Seth Cartwright was on his walkie-talkie, giving commands to unseen associates while urging the crowd away from the car.

But the show wasn't over.

"Mr. Wolfe?" The front doors slid shut behind a blonde wearing one of the Riverboat's dance-hall-girl uniforms. "Mr. Wolfe!"

The woman was running toward the limo, and from this angle, Rebecca couldn't see her face. Dawn, she'd guess. Though Melissa had sported a similar shock of golden ponytail twisted up beneath her feathered cap. A ripple of unease raised the hairs on Rebecca's arms. Surely, Melissa and the boss weren't an item. Had *he* twisted her wrist to the point of nearly breaking it? Rebecca tightened her grip around the steel railing. "Don't be her," she whispered. "Don't be Melissa."

"Teddy!" The blonde pushed her way through the

crowd to the black-haired hunk who stood a head taller than everyone else. "We have to talk."

"Mr. Wolfe cannot—" Shaw reached for the woman, but she pushed him back.

"Get your hands off me!"

"This isn't a good time." Teddy smiled down at the woman, dispersing the crowd with a royal wave, refusing to acknowledge the high-pitched demand in her voice.

"I won't be put off any longer," she argued. "There are things we need to discuss. We have to decide…"

Rebecca lost the next few lines of conversation as the chattering onlookers approached, returning to the casino. She couldn't very well tell them to pipe down without giving herself away. But even though the words were lost, there was still plenty to see up by the limo.

Teddy Wolfe's smile vanished. Angry words to Shaw and Seth kept them at a distance. Teddy's handsome face twisted into an ugly frown before he whispered something to the woman. When she would have slapped his face, he dropped the briefcase and grabbed her arm. With the dangling attaché banging into the blonde's side, he palmed the back of her head and pulled her up onto her toes for a savage kiss.

The woman struggled at first, but then her beating fists stilled and she wound her arms around his neck. The briefcase came to rest atop the woman's bustle as he wrapped her in an embrace. When he finally lifted his head, the bright smile had returned, and the woman's words were low-pitched and inaudible.

Shaw McDonough's words were louder and

harsher. "You cannot be late, Mr. Wolfe. The London office is expecting a wire transfer and your report. Get rid of her."

"I have until midnight, right?" Teddy asked over the blonde's head. A perplexed Shaw nodded. Teddy retrieved the briefcase by the handle. "Then that gives us twenty minutes."

In one smooth move, he stuffed the woman into the back of the limo, climbed in behind her and shut the door himself. With a crude curse and a shake of his head, Shaw reached for the door handle. But Teddy had locked it behind him. With sotto voce orders of his own, Shaw spoke to Seth, then shooed the driver back behind the wheel before climbing into the front seat beside him. After a quick scan of the parking lot, Seth tapped the roof of the car, giving them the clearance to leave. Rebecca could smell the burning rubber as they sped away toward the lights of downtown Kansas City.

Thank God she'd never been involved in a tumultuous relationship like that one.

But her relief was short-lived as an unseen magnetic pull drew her focus back to Seth Cartwright.

She was in no position to judge. *Tumultuous* was the only adjective she could come up with to describe the way she and Seth interacted. But then, theirs wasn't a relationship. They certainly weren't lovers. They'd never dated. She couldn't even count him as a friend.

As her thoughts grew more unsettling, Rebecca summoned the reporter inside her—a far safer bet than thinking as a woman had ever been for her—and followed the limo's red taillights until they disap-

peared. Just what was the blonde's relationship with
Teddy Wolfe? Who was she? And most important,
what secrets could she share about him?

Once the limousine had turned out of sight, Seth
clipped his walkie-talkie onto his belt. He pulled back
the front of his jacket and splayed his fingers at his
waist, a lone figure standing at the peak of the gangplank. His chest expanded with a deep, controlled
breath, creating a powerful silhouette. There was
nothing soft about that man. No hint of a smile. No
chink in his armor. Rebecca watched him make a slow
360-degree turn, surveying the cars and riverbank, the
lights and shadows. Ever watchful. Always on guard.

Like a cop. Or a man with something to hide.

A nagging bit of intuition demanded she make sense
of everything she'd observed. But before the realization could take hold, Seth paused, peering into the
darkness of the deck where she stood.

Rebecca flattened her back against the steel brace
and held her breath. The man wasn't psychic, too, was
he? Sure, she'd been thinking about him. Watching him
along with everything else. But a muscle-bound goon
like that having a sixth sense? Freaky coincidence.
Nothing more. *Look away, already,* she silently pleaded.
A swoosh of breeze from the water below caught her hair
and swirled the loose tendrils around her face. Rebecca
cursed inside her head. The movement would surely
catch his attention. But no, Seth lost interest in her particular shadow and his gaze moved on. By the time she
risked stealing a breath and taming her hair inside her
fist, the Riverboat's Chief of Security was heading back

inside, quickly crossing the gangplank in a loose, purposeful stride.

Rebecca's noisy sigh of relief ended with a shaky smile. She'd survived her night. Resolving to look further into identifying Teddy's lady friend—and finding out whether the woman needed protection or a shrink or a new best friend to tell all her troubles to—Rebecca turned to walk around to the bar.

A flare of light against the bulkhead behind her stopped her in her tracks.

A big man with a long black ponytail and chiseled features indicating his Indian heritage blew out a puff of smoke from his long cigarette. As he unfolded himself from his casual stance against the wall, Rebecca recognized him as the pit boss whom she swore had been following her around the casino earlier. She dropped her gaze to his badge, but it was too dark to read a name.

"What are you lookin' at?" was all he said before stomping his smoke out on the deck and taking a menacing step toward her.

Rebecca instinctively backed away.

His teeth flashed in a momentary smile. Or was it a sneer?

"I wasn't—" Rebecca nixed the impulse to defend herself. She pulled herself up to her full height, though even if she'd worn her high heels, she had no chance of topping him. "Are you following me?" she demanded.

But he wasn't interested in any explanation. And he damn sure wasn't going to hang around to answer any questions.

"You were a lucky woman. Tonight." He bumped

her shoulder as he walked past, knocking her aside half a step even though there was plenty of room for them both on the deck.

Spooked by his silent presence and frightening strength, Rebecca spun around and made sure he entered the casino. A chill gripped her lungs, making her breath come in a ragged gasp.

What was that about?

How long had he been in the shadows with her?

Alone with her?

Was he watching the scene at the limo? The crowd? The water lapping against the Riverboat's side as it flowed past?

Was he watching *her?*

And was he talking about her luck at the tables? Or something more sinister?

How could she have been so wrapped up in spying on Teddy Wolfe and stewing over Seth Cartwright that she hadn't even noticed him?

Reaching for the one source of calm and comfort she could find, Rebecca pulled her father's ring into her fist. "Where were you, Daddy?" she whispered.

She shook her head, embarrassed that she'd given voice to her fear.

These aren't all nice people around here, Seth had warned.

Maybe she had reason to be afraid.

She didn't have a name for the big Indian. But she had a face. A description.

He looked like the kind of man who could kill another.

Chapter Four

The sunshine beaming through the front window of Pearl's Diner was as warm on Rebecca's skin as the mug of coffee she cradled between her hands. Along with the fragrant brew, a big breakfast of French toast and fruit had gone a long way toward reviving her energy and chasing away the chill that lingered inside her after one too many run-ins with unfriendlies at the Riverboat last night.

When the bell over the diner's front door chimed, she looked up. In the bright light of day, she let a real smile crease her face as she greeted the robust man with the silver hair. John Kincaid had been a fraternity brother of her father's back at Mizzou. The two had remained friends for years—and had even formed a working relationship of sorts.

Though Rebecca didn't see John as often as she had when her father was alive, her affection for the older man hadn't diminished. She eagerly slipped out of the booth to accept a hug that swallowed her up and lifted her off the floor.

When her toes touched linoleum again, John

grinned. Busy schedules and different priorities might have kept them apart, but nothing about his charm had changed. "Good grief, Rebecca, you're more gorgeous than ever. A real sight for sore eyes."

"Flatterer."

"Will it get me anywhere?" he teased.

"You wish."

He laid a hand over his wounded heart. "Ah, if I were thirty years younger."

Rebecca laughed as she sat and poured hot coffee into the mug she'd already ordered for him. She hadn't bothered with makeup this morning, and wore nothing more seductive than a tank top, jeans and flip-flops. But she appreciated his sense of humor. "If you were thirty years younger, I wouldn't have even been born yet."

"Ouch." He unbuttoned his blazer and slipped into the seat across from her. "Good thing my wife will still have me."

"Good thing."

The harmless banter reminded her of her father, and how caring could be expressed without using the actual words. John had been a myth from her father's stories until they'd moved to Kansas City and she'd finally gotten to meet the man Reuben Page had held in such high regard. With their own sons nearly grown, John and his wife, Susan, had taken to Rebecca as though she was a favorite niece. With her mother gone and Reuben so involved with his work, Rebecca had gladly let them into her heart as extended family.

The man sitting across from her now had just one tiny little flaw.

John Kincaid was a cop.

But that was precisely the trait she intended to take advantage of this morning.

"So what do I call you now?" she asked, averting her gaze from the brass-and-blue-enamel badge clipped to his belt. "Detective? Captain?"

"John will do just fine. Though there's a chance it might be deputy commissioner soon."

"Really? You're moving up in the world. Congratulations."

"That's strictly off the record, you know. But I am one of the three finalists being considered for the position." Rebecca knew from the Baby Jane Doe murder case that, sadly, the second in command of the Kansas City Police Department's administrative division was no longer able to fulfill his duties. John stirred sugar into his coffee. "I'm sure it's only by virtue of the fact that I've been around since Methuselah that I'm even in the running."

"Don't be so modest. You'll get the promotion because you're good at your job and you've earned the respect of the men and women in your command."

John shrugged off the compliment and sipped the steaming brew. He adjusted the position of the mug on the tabletop before speaking again. "I thought you'd been avoiding me since we moved Reuben's death to the cold-case files. Thought maybe you held it against me."

Maybe she had. A little.

"It's not your fault." She blamed the detectives division—homicide and the major case squad, in particular—for giving up.

They had the bullet from her father's brain, but no gun to match it to. They had the key to an empty bus locker. Nearly a dozen suspects her father had profiled in his column over the years had motive, but they'd all alibied out. The notes from his last story pointed to organized crime coming to Kansas City via investments along the Missouri River. But there'd been no evidence to back up Reuben's suspicions about Wolfe International and bribes to the economic development committee. The connection to Dani Ballard's murder had even run cold. Traces of the slain woman's blood had been found on Reuben's clothes, but his body had deteriorated too far before being discovered for the forensic lab to determine whether he'd fired the gun or picked up the blood after Dani's death.

She had a blurred, distorted map, copied from her father's palm, locked in a leather notebook inside her glove compartment. A map she'd spent hours trying to make sense of, but that the investigators had dismissed as useless scribbles.

KCPD should have kept trying.

John reached across the table to squeeze her hand and pull her from the morbid spiral of her thoughts. "Trust me, if we get any kind of lead, I'll reopen the case personally and pursue it until we put the murdering bastard behind bars."

"I know, John." She squeezed back. "I know you'd help me if you could."

She was about to give her dutch uncle an opportunity to do just that.

"I need some information."

"For the paper? You know we have a press liaison for—"

"It's personal."

"Oh?" John's expression furrowed with concern. "Are you in some kind of trouble?"

"No." Not yet. Rebecca pulled away and straightened against the vinyl seat. "I need to ask you about a man."

"Really." His frown eased into a wink-wink smile. "Sue and I have been wondering when you'd meet someone who could finally distract you from your career." But he sat back, mirroring her posture, when he saw that she hadn't invited him to breakfast to discuss boyfriends. "If it has to do with an open case, you know I can't discuss it with you unless I get clearance from—"

"It's about a cop. An ex-cop. I just need to know more about this guy."

John's gaze narrowed, silently probing for the reasons behind her request. "Who's the guy?"

"Seth…Cartwright." The name hadn't gotten any easier to say.

"The commissioner's boy?"

Rebecca could think of several choice descriptors for the Riverboat's Chief of Security, but *boy* wasn't one of them. "He's the one. Do you know him?"

The jovial uncle became Captain Kincaid of the north-town precinct. "I know *of* him."

Gray-green eyes, honed with suspicion, and a controlled strength that had left no bruises following last night's encounter, were as clear in her memory as the man sitting across from her now. Succinct as Seth's warnings to steer clear of the Riverboat had been, there was an underlying quality of justice about a man who would recruit her to befriend an abused woman. She'd seen real regret in his eyes and heard frustration in his voice—he'd help Missy Teague himself if he could. But something was preventing him from doing so. Something like working on another case that could be jeopardized if he made Missy a priority?

Sounded like the cop-to-the-bone Cartwright family she knew—not a henchman for the mob.

"Is he still a cop?" Rebecca asked, half hoping, half dreading John's answer.

"Now why would you want to know that?" But he could see she wouldn't be put off by any diversionary questions. "I've seen his name on the probation list. First, he had desk duty, but now I think he's on leave with pay. I hear he's got a gambling problem."

"That's ridiculous. He works in a casino."

"A lot of cops moonlight. Probably how he got himself into trouble."

"I didn't think security personnel were allowed to gamble."

"Well, I can only speak to what I've heard." John braced his elbows on the table and leaned forward. "How do you know Cartwright? And how do you know he works in a casino?"

Rebecca hedged. "I met him on some interviews with the commissioner. He was running interference." That sounded like a gracious enough way to explain rolling around the commissioner's front yard with the man.

"Why ask about him now?"

Because he's getting in the way of my investigation? Because he's a thorn that sticks under my skin just deep enough to keep me awake at night? Everything about Seth Cartwright was pure male, from the short clip of his hair to the thick soles of his shoes. Coiled strength. Deep voice. Spare use of words. Quick actions and decisions. Emotions buried deep down inside and revealed in quick bursts that alternately surprised and annoyed her.

But square jaw and muscular pecs aside, she couldn't shake the image of the lonely centurion from the parking lot last night. She'd seen a young man who'd witnessed and done things that had aged him beyond his years. A man living with dangers she'd only written about.

A man whose isolation matched her own.

No. She and Seth Cartwright were not alike. She felt no empathy for him. No compassion. Rebecca plucked the unexpected emotions from her mind. "So you won't tell me if he's still working for KCPD or not?"

"No. I won't."

"Because I'm a reporter and KCPD has something top secret going on at the Riverboat Casino?"

"Because I can't." A sigh eased gentle concern back into his expression. "If Detective Cartwright is on probation, then he's done something he shouldn't have. Police brutality. Compromising an investigation. Sexual harassment. Those are just some possibilities. The fact that he hasn't been fired or put back on active duty means Internal Affairs is still looking for answers."

"I guess I'll have to get in line to find them, then."

"Take some advice from an old family friend?"

He could give it. But Rebecca would decide whether or not to take it. "Sure."

"Stay away from Cartwright. He's trouble."

"I KNEW THAT WOMAN was nothing but trouble." Seth pressed two fingers to his wrist and timed his pulse. But how much of the elevated count could he attribute to his afternoon run through Swope Park, and how much was due to the leggy brunette who had more guts than sense and the most unique shade of golden-brown eyes that he'd ever seen on a woman?

Cooper Bellamy, the detective ghosting him on this undercover assignment, stretched his long legs, preparing to join Seth for the second mile of his run. "Hey, I'm just telling you what Captain Kincaid said to me. Looks like your arch-nemesis, Lois Lane, has been asking about you."

Seth flexed his neck to stay loose. "She's tight with Captain K.?"

"Old family friend, it sounds like."

Coop was as laid back as Seth was tightly wound these days. They met as needed, away from the River-boat and its crew, to trade information. Seth's partner from KCPD's vice squad was his one link to the real world. His distant backup. His only means of communication with the rest of the department and John Kincaid's organized crime unit that had recruited them from the Fourth Precinct because of his father's connections to the gambling world.

"So what did the captain say?" Seth asked.

Pulling a Royals ball cap backward over his clean-shaven head, Coop gave a nod and the two of them started out on a jog along the tree-lined road. "He tried to warn her off. Said you were no good."

Seth winced at the well-rehearsed lie that hit a little

too close to the truth these days. He picked up the pace. "Maybe I *am* no good."

Coop easily matched his speed. "Maybe she's got a thing for bad boys."

"Nah, it's not like that."

"If you say so."

"I do." Seth punched his fists in a boxing pattern as he ran, so as to work his upper body, too. "Trust me, the Amazon princess is after a story. Those legs and that hair are just tools she uses to get what she wants. You can't trust her. There's not one genuine word that comes out of her mouth you can believe in."

"But you've noticed the legs and hair." And the eyes. Why didn't Coop mention the eyes? Hell. Why was Seth even thinking about them? "What is she, Greek descent? Italian?"

"How would I know?"

"You could ask her."

"I'm not asking her anything." Especially when every conversation between them seemed to end up with the two of them in close quarters. Where he could smell her spicy perfume. Feel her heat. Know the shape of that long, lean body. Seth peeled off his T-shirt as they ran and tucked it into the back of his shorts. June seemed to be unusually hot and muggy this year. "She's gonna throw a monkey wrench into our investigation. I can feel it."

Coop grinned. "You know, every time you have a run-in with Rebecca Page, you go on and on about her."

"'Cause she's a pain in the ass."

At twenty-nine, Coop was two years older than

Seth. But Seth always felt like the older, wiser partner until his wise-cracking buddy shared one of his surprising insights into people. Like now. "You don't talk this much about any other woman, with the exception of your sister and mom. Yet here you are, going on about—what did you call her?—the Amazon princess?—again."

That was an uncomfortable observation. "What are you saying?"

"I'm just saying she pushes your buttons."

"Not in a good way."

"You wish she did, though."

Coop towered over Seth by half a foot. But he knew damn well that his short and scrappy self could take the big guy down if he had to. "Do you want to finish this run?"

"Easy, boy." Of course, Coop could talk his way out of just about anything. Even Seth's testy moods. "All right, I'm switching topics. Anything new on the money-laundering at the casino?"

Work. Fine. Good. Seth could handle that. "Wolfe left the Riverboat with a hundred grand last night. Said it was a bank deposit from this week's profits, but there was no paperwork."

"I hear he's hosting a big poker tournament next weekend. Maybe that's his personal stake," Coop suggested.

They cleared the trees and crossed the street to run the sidewalk encircling one of the park's lakes. "Only if Daddy wired him the money from London. Wolfe's personal bank account is in the hole."

"You think he's skimming profits? Or running

through some drug money and claiming it as casino winnings before sending it back to Teddy, Senior?"

Seth shook his head. "I know the drug money's coming in. But I haven't been able to get the books away from Kelleher long enough to see where all of it is going out. Maybe *he's* the one doctoring them."

"Or he's noticed the discrepancies, too, and is trying to figure them out."

Seth's first impression of Daniel Kelleher was that he was a good guy, caught up with the wrong people. But how could he go into business with Wolfe and not know there were some shady dealings going down? He'd been involved with the Riverboat project back when he first served as an advisor to the city's economic development committee. Would he have been such a strong advocate for Wolfe International bringing a new casino to K.C. if he'd known about the company's suspected criminal activities? Or was that precisely why Kelleher had worked so tirelessly to convince Kansas City to welcome the Wolfe company?

Of course, Seth's own father had invested in the Riverboat, though he still hadn't figured out how his debt-ridden dad had gotten his hands on investment money. What he earned through a year of hard work, he could gamble away in one night of bad bets. Even his architectural fees for redesigning the *Commodore* didn't add up to that kind of cash. Austin Cartwright's explanation about "finally picking the big game" just didn't sit right. But how could he accuse his own father of being guilty of anything besides being a lousy dad?

Seth rolled his shoulders, shaking off that pesky train of thought. They were discussing Daniel Kelleher.

"Didn't he have a run-in with the law a few years back? Suspected insurance fraud? I remember a string of arson fires."

"I'll look into it." They'd nearly completed the mile-long circle. "Any luck hacking into the computers?"

"Everything I've accessed thus far has been legit. Between Wolfe, Kelleher and McDonough's codes, the rest is pretty well encrypted. I'd love to get one of our tech experts to hack into the system."

"They're working on it, but Wolfe International operates off its own server, and remote access is tricky without alerting them to the investigation."

Seth puffed out a curse. "Maybe you could just get me a list of all their passwords."

Coop laughed. Yeah, like that miracle was gonna happen. "I'll see what I can do. Anything else?"

"Find out if Rebecca Page has any tie-in to the Riverboat. She says she's there to do a history article, but I'm not buying it."

"Back to the intrepid reporter, eh?"

"It's work-related, Coop."

"Uh-huh. I can get her phone number for you, too, if you want."

Was that a wink? "Is there some reason why I agreed to let you be my liaison to the department while I'm working this assignment?"

"Sure. You're too damn serious and I make you laugh." Seth rolled his eyes. "Because you've been blackballed by the department as part of your cover and I'm the only one who'll still put up with you?" Seth slowed to a walk and pulled his shirt out to mop the sweat from his face and chest. Coop halted beside him, his mouth open to breathe deeply as he bent forward to brace his hands on his knees. "I got it. It's the only way you can keep an eye on me so I don't hit on your twin sister."

Seth snorted at that one. "Okay, pal, now you've gone too far." He tapped Coop's shoulder with a trio of fake punches. "My sister, Sarah, is off…limits…to you."

"Ooh. Ow. Ow." Coop stood tall and palmed the top of Seth's head, shoving him out to arm's length. "Take that."

"Don't think so." And the race was on.

Seth's legs pumped faster than Coop's loping stride, keeping them evenly matched as they charged toward the parking lot. It was rare to feel the normalcy of a couple of guys giving each other grief, trusting that— for a few minutes—someone had his back. Seth relished the laughter and friendship.

"Maybe we should double date sometime," shouted Coop as they neared his truck.

"Who?"

"Sweet little Sarah and me, and you and Rebecca."

Him with Rebecca? The idea was enough to make Seth pull up half a step and lose the race.

"WHAT the hell?"

The man tossed back the covers and swore, roused from a deep sleep by the buzzing of the telephone. He pushed away the woman snoring atop his chest and sat up to swing his legs off the side of the bed. He turned on a lamp, picked up his smokes and checked the caller ID.

"Damn." His caller had no consideration for the time difference across the ocean. That it was the middle of the night here, that he'd just gotten laid and planned to get laid again before tonight's partner left in the morning, didn't matter to the caller.

When this man phoned, answering was the only option. But that didn't mean he had to like it.

He pulled out a long, thin cigar, lit it and inhaled a soothing drag to calm his resentment before answering.

"Mr. Wolfe."

"Good morning." There was no point in mentioning that it was two o'clock at night here in Missouri. Theodore Wolfe, Sr., didn't care. So he took another draw off the imported tobacco and waited for his instructions. The boss got right to the point. "I was reading the numbers this morning. I didn't make the investment I did in Kansas City to turn measly profits like this. I should be seeing reports of twice this much."

"It's not my job to fix the numbers," he pointed out.

"No. But it is your job to stay on top of things there. Is it a problem with our distributors not turning in their quotas?"

They funneled in enough drug money from an eight-state area to finance a small country. "I keep our people in line when they don't pony up the cash. That's not the problem."

"Is it the casino, then? I understood that those big poker tournaments gave us plenty of opportunity to bring in large sums of cash to launder through the company."

Funny how a man could annoy him all the way from

London. "We're using the same set-up you have in place there. The money comes in, it shows up in our books as legitimate payouts, we take our cut and then send the rest on to you."

"No one's skimming more than their cut, are they?"

As if he was going to answer that one. "Like I said. I don't fix the books."

His boss went through a list of numbers and possibilities that should have interested him more than they did. But the woman was stirring in the bed behind him, and his body immediately hardened with the need to take her again.

"Is Teddy the problem?"

Give the man a cheroot.

The naked man in the bed smiled at the tone of paternal disappointment. "Your son is a real pro at getting customers to the casino and recruiting big players for the private games."

"But…?"

He was paid to tattle. "He's got a big game coming up soon, but I don't think Teddy's mind is on business."

"Is it another woman?" He didn't have to answer that one. But Daddy cursed in that proper, damning British way of his. "I'll talk to him myself."

He nearly wasted a mouthful of smoke when the woman's fingertip traced the length of his spine. For an instant he battled between the desire to roll her onto her back or to slap her hand away for initiating something before he was ready.

But he could do neither until he finished the call. "Is that all you needed?"

"No."

Of course not. There was always more to be done for Wolfe International. He put out his cigar and eyed the gun, the knife and the tiny remote control trigger lying beside the ashtray on the nightstand. They were the tools of his trade. And he used each one with equal precision.

"What do you want me to do?"

Chapter Five

Seth knew the instant Rebecca Page walked into the suite of security offices.

The atmosphere changed.

It wasn't just the extra buzz of voices out in the reception area that caught his ear. Instead, he likened it to the electric charge that built up in the air when a storm was brewing.

And the long-legged lightning bolt was certain to strike.

Seth looked up from the printout of faces on the bad check report he'd been reviewing with casino personnel and sought out Rebecca Page. His office door was propped open and he could see straight over the row of carpeted cubicles to the front desk.

There she stood, smiling and chatting with the receptionist. With her long curly hair swooped back into a loose ponytail and her face scrubbed of the heavy makeup she'd worn last night, Rebecca almost looked like a different woman. Innocent—as though she didn't have a crafty bone in her body. Pretty in a way that made him wish they didn't share any twisted history—

that he could meet her in a bar or through a friend and enjoy her company without any of the baggage that tainted his mistrust of her.

But Seth knew better. She was as driven in her pursuit of the news as he was in his pursuit of the bad guys. And no matter what insight his partner, Coop, thought he had about Seth's attraction to the reporter, a flare of hormones at the sight of her brushing one of those long corkscrew curls off her neck did not mean he wanted to get closer to Rebecca Page in any way, shape or form.

He was working here. Making nice with the men he was investigating. Digging up facts.

The tricky part was that Seth had a feeling Rebecca was doing the same damn thing.

As though she was feeling the same electric current that had drawn her to his attention, Rebecca looked up from the papers she was signing and locked on to his assessing gaze. Neither the distance nor the activity in the room between them could lessen the impact of those tawny eyes meeting his. She had no acknowledging nod or hint of a smile for him. But the soft pink that stained her cheeks was evidence enough that she was as aware of him as he was of her.

Or maybe just as suspicious.

Damn. Now there was an unsettling thought. Seth looked away and continued going through the motions of his weekly security briefing.

But his thoughts were still at the front reception desk. He bought Rebecca's history-article excuse about as much as he believed she had put his mother's safety and wellbeing ahead of breaking the story on one of the most notorious murder cases in Kansas City history. A year ago, Rebecca had been all about getting the exclusive on his mother's stalker and finally solving the Baby Jane Doe murder.

And now, after mucking through the trenches on that career-making story, she willingly resigned herself to researching the history of an old boat?

A sickening possibility twisted in the pit of his stomach.

She'd already been talking to Captain Kincaid about him. What if *he* was the story Rebecca was really after here? Life in an Undercover Cop's World. Yeah. Just the kind of headline that could get him killed. Did she resent his efforts to protect his own mother by impeding her job that much? Or was she so focused on building a success-ful career that the consequences of her actions be damned?

Or was there a less volatile, more innocent side to Rebecca Page that could be satisfied with a story on the *Commodore?* She had seemed truly concerned about helping Melissa Teague. While his hands were tied with his Wolfe International assignment, he'd like to see a strong advocate in Melissa's corner.

Maybe he should ratchet the protective antagonism down a notch and try making nice with Rebecca. Get to know her. Find out what she was really after here. If he could pretend he enjoyed working for the mob, he could surely manage to get along with one diehard journalist.

He sought Rebecca out a second time. Now, she was lined up in front of a blue screen so the receptionist, LaTonya, could take her picture for a staff ID card.

So she was really going to go through with this. Researching a story under an assumed name. *His* story? On his turf? With these people?

"Anything else, Cartwright? I've got things to do."

People like this guy.

Seth slowly pulled his attention back to the man sitting across the desk from him. Richard "Ace" Longbow. Built like a mountain and possessing all the warmth of a glacier, the Native American pit boss had already earned a place on Seth's arrest list.

Though on paper Ace had been hired away from a casino in South Dakota to supervise the Riverboat's gaming tables, Seth had already witnessed more than one instance of his real purpose here. He was one of Teddy Wolfe's thugs—meant to and able to intimidate business associates and hired help who didn't keep their end of whatever bargain they'd struck with Teddy and Wolfe International: gamblers who couldn't pay their markers in the private poker games Teddy hosted in his suite of rooms upstairs, drug dealers who didn't meet their quota of cash to be laundered through the Riverboat's accounting system, ambitious employees or players who simply pissed off Teddy Wolfe for any number of reasons.

Using violence and blackmail as his stock in trade, Ace Longbow excelled at whatever assignment Teddy gave him.

Seth should know. As proof of his own loyalty to the Wolfes, he'd been ordered to *enforce* a couple of house rules himself. Without the legal sanction of his Gaming Commission security clearance. Yeah. He could see that blurb in one of Rebecca Page's stories.

Focus. Ace Longbow was definitely not a man around whom he could let down his guard.

But he couldn't arrest Ace. Not yet. Not without tipping his hand. Seth and KCPD were after the big players. They wanted Teddy Wolfe, Wolfe International—and an unknown partner who seemed to really be calling the shots around here, despite Teddy's efforts to rule the roost. Ultimately, they were after the Kansas City link to European mobster Theodore Wolfe, Sr. And hell, if they could bring down Teddy, Sr., while they were at it, that'd be the icing on the cake.

"That'll be it, Ace." He scooted the stack of photocopies across the desk. "Pass the flyers out to your dealers and let me or one of my men know if any of them come in. It'll be cash only if they want to play."

"Got it." Ace rose from his seat, buttoned his jacket and nodded to the others in the room. "Let's go."

Seth stood as well. There was no way he could match Ace in stature, but he could more than beat Teddy's thug in the attitude department. This was *his* meeting, *his* office. Ace Longbow wasn't in command. Seth acknowledged each shift manager and security supervisor in the room before dismissing them himself. "We're done here. Make it a good one."

Following the group out, Seth paused to sort through the messages on his assistant's desk. But he wasn't really interested in returning anyone's call at the moment. It was just an excuse to get closer to the front end of the room to observe how Rebecca interacted with the staff here. Somehow she managed to be completely professional and completely charming at the same time.

What an act. He wished he could put a microphone on her and track what she was really up to, the same way he'd bugged the strategic offices on board the Riverboat. But he'd have to content himself with observation.

She was quickly bonding with the receptionist. Apparently, she'd already made friends with one of the shift managers, as he stopped to share a conversation with her. It was a subtle trick, really, to pull more information from the people she met than she revealed herself.

It was a trick Seth used every single day on this assignment.

The only person who didn't seem to think she already fit into the Riverboat family was Ace. The big Indian paused when he reached the reception area. He stopped and stood there, unmoving, staring at Rebecca until her conversation faltered and her gaze darted up to his. Though no words were exchanged, Ace shrugged as soon as the contact was made, then he looked away and strode past her out the door.

The messages crumpled inside Seth's fist. That smug son of a bitch. What kind of power play was that? Did he recognize Rebecca? Was that his lame attempt at flirting? Seth knew that some women went for that stoic type. Quiet, needy Melissa Teague once had, apparently. But she and Ace had ceased to be an item long before Seth had gotten his first job at the casino more than eight months ago. Or was there something else going on between Teddy's henchman and the incognito reporter that Seth was completely out of the loop on?

Seth dropped the messages on the desk and crossed the length of the office before Rebecca could fix her game face back into place. As much as she clashed with him, messing with Ace Longbow wasn't an option he'd allow. He spared her a glance and passed right on by, heading out the door in time to see Ace flag down Teddy Wolfe and Dawn Kingsley coming up the grand staircase.

Despite Dawn's whine of protest, Teddy dismissed his current affair with a kiss on her cheek and a swat on her bottom, ordering her back down to the main floor. Then the two men went into Teddy's private suite on the opposite side of the landing, closing the door behind them.

The instinct to follow and find out what the taciturn Indian had to say jolted through the muscles in Seth's legs. But, controlling the urge with the clench of his fists at his sides, he hung back out of sight in the arch of another doorway. Barging into the boss's quarters would require a far better explanation than his desire to find out what Ace was so keen to report.

He'd have to rely on the voice-activated microphones hidden inside Teddy's office to record anything important. He'd pull the tape and listen to it later tonight. Ace's silent interchange with Rebecca might not mean a thing beyond the big dog staking out his territory. But this scrappy little watchdog intended to keep a close eye on things.

Whether or not that impromptu meeting was important, standing in the hallway wouldn't get him any answers. He'd take a cue from Rebecca herself and go straight to the source.

Time to put his get-friendly-with-the-enemy
strategy into effect.

Rebecca was at the front counter, pointing to the
card in the receptionist, LaTonya's, hand as Seth reen-
tered the security reception area. Apparently, her paperwork had hit a glitch.

"Is this the only form of ID you have, Miss
Poochman?" LaTonya asked. "No credit cards? No
school or state photo ID?"

"No. Isn't my license all I need? I didn't have any
problem filling out the tax forms in Mr. Kelleher's
office."

"For security, we normally require two."

The woman could sure think on her feet. Rebecca
leaned in over the counter, twisting her face into a
pitiful woman-to-woman plea. "I'm recently divorced.
You know how hard it is to get all the documentation
changed back from my married name. Isn't there some
way you can fudge—?"

He'd seen enough of the show.

"It's all right, LaTonya. Let me see that driver's
license." Seth joined Rebecca at the counter, resting his
forearms on the ledge beside hers, standing close
enough to feel her flinch against him when they
touched.

She clutched her oversize shoulder bag beneath her
arm and scooted farther down the counter, leaving her
orangey-ginger scent and some well-aimed visual
barbs behind her as she went.

Seth ignored both the enticement and the taunt as
he examined the clearly fake license. Kelleher's office
had approved this? He ought to reward LaTonya for

having such a sharp eye. Instead, he handed the card back to the receptionist. "I know Miss Poochman. I'll vouch for her. We're old friends."

"Fr—?"

Seth glanced over at the slight gape of Rebecca's mouth. The image of those full, pink, parted lips sucker-punched him right below the belt. He'd never considered kissing Rebecca Page before. Shouldn't be considering it now. Shouldn't be considering it at all. Lifting his appreciative gaze to the prickly glare a few inches higher up on her face reminded him why.

Silently laughing at the joke his hormones kept trying to pull on him, he reached out and touched the soft point of her chin, nudging her mouth shut. "We've known each other a long time," he added, inviting Rebecca to play along with the ruse. "Right, Poochman?"

Those pink lips twisted into a tight smile. "Right, Cartwright."

"Oh. I didn't realize. Sure thing, Mr. Cartwright." LaTonya thrust her hand over the counter to shake Rebecca's hand. "Welcome to the Riverboat. I'll download the photo with your information. Your ID card will take about five minutes to process. You'll need it to gain access to private personnel areas. Of course, the counting room is off limits, as is the—"

"Thanks, LaTonya. I'll explain the details to her while she waits. When her card's ready, we'll be in my office, catching up." Seth brushed his fingers across Rebecca's back, damning the instant leap of heat in each cell as he inadvertently found the narrow strip of exposed skin between the hem of her sleeveless blouse and the waistband of her hip-hugging khakis. She sucked in her breath, breaking the contact without physically moving away. Rebecca was either ticklish, repulsed by his touch—or battling the same unwanted attraction he was.

That was *not* the kind of friendly alliance he was hoping to make with the woman.

"This way." Moving his hand to a more neutral position, he guided her around the counter to the rear of the suite.

As soon as he closed his office door behind them, Rebecca shot to the center of the room and whirled around. "*You'll* vouch for me?"

In his office—out of earshot, and more important, out of any security-camera shot—was the only place he'd let this heart-to-heart of tempers and truths happen. Seth circled around his desk. "Trust me, Miss *Poochman,* I'm not doing you any favors. Where did you come up with a name like that?"

"Poochman was one of my dogs growing up."

"You should have stuck with your mother's maiden name." He sat in his chair and pointed to a seat across the desk. "You really got that homemade license past Kelleher?"

"Actually, he was on the phone when I turned in my wage forms. He only saw a photocopy."

Seth shook his head and wondered how long it would take a real Chief of Security—one who wasn't being paid by Teddy Wolfe to overlook discrepancies like the credentials he'd just okayed—to throw Miss *Poochman* out on her pretty little butt.

Meanwhile, Rebecca perched on the edge of her

chair, clutching that big black shoulder tote in her lap. "Last night, you couldn't get rid of me fast enough. Today you're smoothing the process to get me hired? What's with the Jekyll and Hyde routine?"

A real Chief of Security—a real cop—*he*—wouldn't put up with any more of these games. "What's the deal between you and Ace Longbow?" he countered.

"Who?"

"The big Indian who stared you down a few minutes ago. Do you think he recognized you from the paper?"

Her posture softened and the fight went out of her tone. "I don't know how he could. I sure don't…know him."

Seth gauged the hesitance in her answer. What was he missing here? He rested his elbows on the desktop, fisting his hands together and leaning toward her. "Any reason why he'd report your arrival to Teddy Wolfe?"

Her eyebrows arched. "He did?"

"I'm not sure. But he went straight from seeing you here into Teddy's office." He uncurled a fist and pointed to the calculating animation he could already see returning to her eyes. "Just so you know, Teddy Wolfe is strictly off-limits to you. He can't help you with your history article."

"I'd love to ask him what it was about the *Commodore* that inspired him to buy it."

Seth pushed to his feet. "In a pig's eye. You're a crime-beat reporter. If you think Teddy is up to something he shouldn't be, spill it."

She stood as well, mirroring him across the desk. "If you think I'm after your boss, then why did you just ensure that I got a job here?"

"Two words. Melissa Teague."

"I thought if I agreed to help her, you were going to stay off my back."

"No." Seth leaned in. "I just agreed to let you be on the premises. There's hardly any room in this casino where I can't watch what you're up to. So don't try getting any kind of scoop out of Teddy."

Her chin thrust out in that elegant, arrogant tilt. "Taking up voyeurism as a hobby?"

"Doing my job."

"Is it your job to spy on me and overlook whatever's happening to Melissa?" She wrapped her fingers around her wrist in a pointed reminder of Melissa's latest injury. "If you really cared about her, she'd be your focus. Not the history story I'm trying to write. Hasn't anybody else here tried to help her?"

"A lot of folks have a lot of troubles of their own. Either they're so caught up in their own issues that they don't want to see what she's going through, or they're afraid of the consequences if they do step up and get involved."

Rebecca leaned in, close enough that he could have kissed her—if he'd wanted to. Damn, he shouldn't want to. "You're not afraid of anything. Why don't you *get involved?*"

The accusation stung as much as the conflicting signals his body was sending to his brain. Seth pulled back, wisely putting some distance between them. "I've tried. I've filed reports. I've called the crisis center for her—and the police. But unless she presses charges or I catch the son of a bitch in the act myself, there's nothing else I can do."

Her ponytail tumbled over her shoulder as she leaned in another inch—on one of those damned reporter's attacks that had made him so crazy to protect his mother last year. "Filed reports? Pressing charges? That sounds like a cop talking to me. What are you really doing in this place, Cartwright?"

Cripes. Tactical error. Since when the hell did he make slip-ups like that? Especially around a woman as perceptive as Rebecca?

But Seth could go on the offensive, too. He circled the desk, watching her straighten, grow taller, don that invisible armor she wore. "None of your business, Poochman. But as long as you take care of Melissa for me, you can stay. And I'll do everything I can to help you get your story." When he stood right behind her, he brushed the ponytail aside and whispered into her ear. "Until I find out what you're really after. Because you, sweetheart, ain't writin' no history article."

Maybe he'd pushed back a little too hard.

She squeezed the heavy pendant hanging around her neck through the glazed cotton of her blouse. With the other hand, she pushed him away and quickly put the length of the room between them. "Back off, Cartwright."

The words were right but the delivery was all wrong. Rebecca Page, aka Poochman, failing to make direct eye contact was a sure indication that he'd struck a nerve. Or that she was about to tell another lie.

"Mr. Cartwright?" LaTonya knocked on the door, ending the conversation before Seth could figure out which was the right answer.

HE HAD a sister.

Rebecca paused at the entrance to the Cotton Blossom Bar, adjusting the balance of the drinks on her tray as an excuse to observe the hushed argument unfolding over at the craps table.

"I told you to go home." Austin Cartwright snapped the order through tightly clenched teeth. She'd only been here a week, and this was already the third incident she'd witnessed of Austin's obsession with gambling getting him into trouble.

She had a feeling the petite woman standing beside him had seen a lot more than three incidents.

Take away the muscles and the glare, and add a shot of all-American pretty, and the green-eyed blonde was a dead ringer for Seth Cartwright. "Dad, come on. Let's go get some coffee somewhere. Or a late dinner. My treat."

"Why are you here? Did your mother send you because I missed another alimony payment?" He squeezed the hand that rested on his arm before brushing it away. "No, wait. I don't even have that connection to her anymore, do I? She and loverboy are off on an island somewhere, soaking in the sun and laughing behind my back."

Rebecca delivered her first drink and made change, moving closer as the young woman schooled her patience. "Mom and Eli are married now, Dad. They're on their honeymoon."

"So you got stuck with dad duty. Isn't it enough that your brother's got his eye on me 24/7?"

"Dad, can't we take this conversation somewhere more private?"

"No, we can't! I'm in the middle of a streak here." A losing streak, judging by the short stack of chips lined up in front of him. "I'm not leaving the table."

"Mr. Cartwright—"

Both father and daughter ignored the croupier's efforts to get Austin's attention and calm the nervous customers who hadn't already walked away from the table. "Go home, Sarah."

The petite blonde was firmer this time. "Dad, your landlord called me. Since I co-signed the lease, *I'm* going to have to pay your rent unless you can get it to him by Friday."

"What?" Austin paused long enough to give his daughter a look that reminded Rebecca of all the times Reuben had been angered and protective on her behalf. "Oh, no, baby, you don't have to do that. That has to be a mistake." He swung his focus back to the table and nodded to the croupier to continue playing. "I'll get the money. I'll pay."

He reached back to touch his daughter's cheek in a tender gesture. There was real love there. Even when it settled on the dysfunctional side of things, that father-daughter connection sparked a tad of envy inside Rebecca, and reminded her how much she missed trading hugs with Reuben. Discussing issues, listening to advice. Even just hanging out with him.

Though her costume hid the ring she always wore, Rebecca pressed her hand to the spot where it rested near her heart. *I miss you, Dad.* If only getting her dad out of a casino before he gambled away his rent money was the problem she had. At least he'd be alive. At least she could tell him she loved him.

"Where's my drink?" Austin snapped, pulling her firmly back into the moment before the tears rubbing like grit beneath her eyelids could overflow.

She blinked away the telltale signs of her grief. "Right here, you old coot."

"Sorry." For a second, he looked appropriately contrite.

But even before she reached the table, he'd turned his focus back to the craps game. Up close, she could hear the rhythmic clacking of plastic hitting plastic as he flipped his last two twenty-dollar chips back and forth between his fingers. He was staring so hard at the green felt board that he didn't even see her holding out his drink.

"C'mon, Hank. I'm feeling lucky. My daughter's here."

His daughter wrapped her hand around his and stilled the chatter of chips. "I don't want you to do that, Dad. Don't use me as an excuse to place that bet."

She tightened her hand and pulled away when he ignored her, too.

"Who's shootin' the dice?"

The ominous bulk of Ace Longbow moved into Rebecca's peripheral vision. Like a dozen curious customers, he hadn't missed the antsy pitch in Austin's voice. He was on his walkie-talkie, speaking so low that she couldn't make out the words. But his expression was clear. A confrontation with Austin in this manic state wouldn't end well.

Whether she was protecting a potential source or another father who could be hurt, Rebecca wasn't sure. But she had every intention of getting to Austin before

Ace did. She turned to face him at the table, using her full back to block Ace's view. "Will you join me out on the deck? I'm due for my break. I'd love to talk some more about the *Commodore*'s blueprints."

"No, I do not want to take a break." He grabbed his drink and downed a third of it in one swallow. "I'm waiting, Hank."

Perhaps teamwork could accomplish what one woman could not. She turned her attention to Austin's daughter, standing on the opposite side. "Hi. I'm Rebecca. A friend of Austin's"

"I'm Sarah."

"Would you like to join us?"

"Do you two mind?" He put his last two chips on the table. "There. On ten to win. Put your bets down, folks. C'mon, Hank, be good to me."

Sarah Cartwright understood Rebecca's invitation was more than an overture of friendship. "Thanks for trying to help, but—"

"Hush, baby."

"Austin." A distinctive British accent startled them all. Teddy. Rebecca had been so focused on avoiding Ace that she hadn't seen him approach. The Riverboat's top dog dropped one hand to the small of her back and squeezed Austin's shoulder with the other. Some day she'd have to study the art of oozing charm while issuing an unmistakable warning. "Is there a problem here?"

"There's no problem." Austin shook him off.

Teddy was still smiling as his hand settled on Austin again. "I let you spend your evenings here to encourage the guests to play, not drive them from the tables."

"We're all having a friendly game here." By *all,* Austin meant one bleary-eyed cowboy and the three of them urging him to leave.

He winced as Teddy's grip tightened. "If I tell you to leave, you leave."

"Just one more round. I owe my daughter some money."

Even as Teddy's hand slid around to the crook of Rebecca's waist, he was smiling down at the woman standing on the opposite side of Austin's stool. "Don't tell me this beautiful woman is your daughter. Thank goodness the ugly genes run on the male side of the family, eh?" He extended his right hand and captured the blonde's fingers in his grip. "I'm Teddy Wolfe. I own the Riverboat. May I have the pleasure?"

With a creepy sense of déjà vu, Rebecca watched him lift the woman's hand to his lips and kiss it. "Sarah Cartwright," she introduced herself.

Rebecca squirmed. Same moves, same lines he'd used on her. No wonder Dawn had jealousy issues.

"Sarah." Teddy rolled the name around his tongue as though he found it and her delicious. Maybe he found her jeans and West Lawn Elementary Staff T-shirt a refreshing contrast to the costumes and fancy duds all around them. "Perhaps I could persuade you and your father to join me for a drink upstairs in my suite."

Sarah's cheeks flooded with color. But she seemed to possess a solid mix of her father's charm and her brother's ability to stand her ground. "I'm not dressed to party tonight. Maybe another time."

"I look forward to it."

"Teddy, stop." Austin finally got up and pulled Sarah away, as though a protective fatherly instinct had finally kicked in. "Not with her."

Though he inclined his head with an agreeable nod, Teddy's fingers pinched at Rebecca's waist. Her startled "Ow" went unacknowledged, unapologized for. Rebecca hugged her tray in front of her, fighting the urge to smack his hand away.

Any other man, any other circumstance… But she had a role to play. If helping Teddy hide his displeasure over being told no would earn her some trust points, and keep her in the conversation long enough to learn something about the way he conducted business, then she'd be his stress doll.

"I am not the one with the problem, Austin. You are in no position to tell me what I can and cannot do."

"She's not part of anything I owe you."

Teddy's grip hurt. Rebecca squirmed but bit her tongue. What did Austin owe Teddy? Money? How much? Loyalty? What did a man have to do to prove his allegiance to Teddy Wolfe? Play the tables? Hustle customers?

Kill a man who was a threat to Wolfe International's survival here in K.C.?

"What you owe me is…" Teddy stopped the threat before Rebecca could learn any secret. He fiddled with his tie, needlessly adjusting its perfect knot while he worked through something inside. Finally, the bruising possession of his hand on her eased its intensity. His handsome smile returned, with all its deceptive charm aimed straight at Sarah Cartwright. "Neither one of us is so crass as to consider a date with your daughter as payment. I can see that she's too much of a lady to allow either one of us even to think it."

"What are you talking about?" Sarah frowned—confused? alarmed?—at the subtle undertones in Teddy's words.

"Nothing, baby." Austin hugged an arm around his daughter and turned her toward the front doors. "We were just leaving."

"Goodnight," Teddy called after Sarah. Though she raised her hand in a hesitant wave, Austin kept moving. "Come back soon. Without the old man."

Once Austin and Sarah reached the hostesses at the front of the casino, Teddy released Rebecca and swatted her bottom. "You'd better get back to work."

Rebecca's momentum carried her forward, bumping her into the craps table. She grabbed the edge and held on, seething with the desire to spin around and slap Teddy's face. That would hardly endear her to the man. But, for her father's sake, she would tolerate the humiliation.

Still, as she gathered up Austin's drink glass and headed back to the Cotton Blossom, Rebecca couldn't help but tilt her gaze and glance from camera mount to camera mount as she passed. Where was Seth Cartwright during all this? Watching the monitors in his office? He'd as good as warned her that he'd be watching her every second she was on Riverboat property. Was that how *he* proved his loyalty to Teddy Wolfe? By turning his head while his employer insulted his father and hit on his sister? And assaulted her? Was the soon-to-be-ex-cop laughing at her own discomfort? Was he hoping enough slimy encounters with Teddy's schmooze-and-use style would drive her away from the story she was after?

Ha. If Seth Cartwright actually thought that, then he didn't know determination. She wasn't leaving the Riverboat until she'd exposed her father's killer.

Twenty minutes later, Rebecca was at the bar, waiting for Tom Sawyer to fill her drink order when Teddy walked into the Cotton Blossom. Ace loomed in the archway behind him, casting an ominous shadow.

Spotting his prey, Teddy buttoned his suit coat and crossed to the tiny blond waitress clearing an empty booth near the center of the room. "Melissa, dear, how are you feeling?"

Empty beer bottles clinked together as Teddy walked up behind her. Even in the dim light of the bar, Rebecca could see the pale cast to Melissa's cheeks as she turned to face him. "I'm all right."

"I heard that you sprained your wrist." He reached for her hand and inspected the brace that she wore. "Is everything healing all right?"

"Don't worry, Teddy." She pulled away and, if Rebecca wasn't mistaken, wiped off his touch on her apron as she turned to resume her work. "I'm not interested in suing for workman's comp."

"Since it's not work-related, there'd be nothing you could do, anyway." To an injured woman, a casual comment like that could be interpreted as a threat. Rebecca tensed—watching, waiting—wondering what she could do to help Melissa. "But that doesn't mean

I don't care about your situation. I'd like to discuss something with you."

Melissa gestured to the noisy tables around them. "We're swamped. Tom needs me."

"It'll only take a minute."

"Maybe I can get away later—"

Melissa visibly jerked as Ace joined them. "It wasn't a request."

Leaving her tray, Rebecca hurried over to try to even up the odds. "You don't have to go with them if you don't want to."

Melissa seemed even more startled by the offer of support than by Ace's threat. She hugged her arms around her stomach, but forced a smile. "It's okay, Rebecca. Just finish this table for me, would you?"

It sure as hell didn't look okay. But Rebecca would grant the one request Melissa asked of her. "No problem."

"We're just going to talk," Teddy insisted. Rebecca didn't believe it. Not for one second. He hooked Melissa's arm through his and brushed past. "Let's go out on the deck. It's such a pleasant evening."

He pushed open the swinging door and ushered Melissa out ahead of him. Her customers completely forgotten, Rebecca hustled after them, intending to keep an eye on her new friend.

But Ace moved surprisingly fast for such a big man, and blocked the exit before she reached it. "This is a private conversation."

"I have customers out there," she tried to reason. It was worth a shot.

Ace's black eyes narrowed. She wasn't getting out to the deck through this door.

She tried again. "Is Mel all right? Did something happen?"

"You sure are curious about a lot of things that don't concern you."

Reason hadn't worked. Compassion hadn't either. She'd try the direct approach. She propped her hands on her hips and tipped her chin. "Somebody nearly broke Melissa's arm. And I have a feeling she's been hurt like that before. You wouldn't know anything about that, would you?"

"If I wanted to break someone's arm, it'd be broken." He crossed his own arms, widening his shoulders to a massive silhouette. "Now get out of my face and leave Mr. Wolfe and his business alone."

Turned away by the immovable object in her path, Rebecca reluctantly went back to work. She cleared Melissa's table, wracking her brain for a way to get around Ace and coming up with nothing that didn't involve stampeding elephants or bazookas. She tried to get Tom's attention, but the bartender was caught up in a hushed conversation on his cell phone.

Seth, where are you? She looked directly into the camera behind the bar. *See this. Protect her,* she silently urged.

Not that long ago, she'd been hurling mute accusations at the man behind the monitors. Now she was turning to her old enemy and asking for help. It was a strange alliance—her and Seth. But there wasn't another soul on this boat who had the strength of his hell-be-damned personality to stand up to men like Ace and Teddy.

Of course, there was the small problem of convincing him to make that stand.

In the meantime, Melissa Teague had to rely on her.

Teddy and Ace left the bar five minutes later, but Melissa didn't reappear. More alarmed than she cared to be, Rebecca wasted no time hurrying outside. She spotted Melissa at a secluded table near the railing, her hands clasped over her stomach, her downturned eyes staring into the river water rushing past beneath her feet.

"Mel?" The other woman sat so still for so long, that, for a moment, Rebecca thought the worst had happened. But then she saw the red-rimmed eyes. *Bastard.* She slipped into the chair beside Melissa, and reached out to rub her arm. Her skin felt chilled to the touch, despite the balmy summer night. "What happened? What did Teddy say to you?"

Melissa lifted her tear-stained face but didn't answer.

"Is he trying to pay you off or talk you out of pressing charges against him?"

"What are you talking about?"

"Pressing charges against Teddy Wolfe. For assaulting you."

She looked stricken by the idea. "Teddy didn't hurt me."

"Are you protecting someone else?"

"Stop it, Rebecca. Stop asking questions." Then, grimacing as though snapping at someone caused her pain, Melissa squeezed Rebecca's hand and pleaded, "I made a mistake, okay? Now I'm trying to fix it. Teddy is helping me fix it."

"By scaring the crap out of you? By making you cry? How does that help?"

"I'm just not feeling well. Stress. Probably my ulcer acting up." Melissa hastily wiped away her tears. Then she inclined her head toward the boisterous trio of customers coming out onto the deck. "You'd better go take care of them. I… I need…" She clutched her stomach and jerked to her feet. "Tell Tom I need to run to the rest room."

As pale as her expression was, Rebecca couldn't offer any kind of argument to make her stay and talk. She was on her feet, following Melissa to the door. "Do you need me to go with you?"

Melissa covered her mouth and shook her head. If her skin lost any more color, she'd faint. "I'll be fine in a minute. Don't leave Tom shorthanded."

Try as she might to get away, Rebecca never got a chance to follow up on Melissa and Teddy's discussion. Tomorrow, she swore—tomorrow she'd find out just what kind of relationship Teddy and Melissa really shared.

But by the end of the night, she just wanted to go home and get some sleep. With her tired feet cushioned in a comfy pair of tennis shoes, and the clingy polyester of her costume exchanged for the cool breathability of denim capris and a ribbed tank-top, Rebecca walked out to her car.

Though the bar and main restaurant had closed at one o'clock, there were still plenty of staff and customers left to cash in chips and tickets and clean up the casino. That meant the lot was still fairly packed with vehicles.

And, despite the influx of money with the casino, this wasn't the best part of town. With the late hour, the limited visibility and the dangerous neighborhood, Rebecca was smart enough to avoid shortcuts and stick to the circles of light cast by the periodic lampposts. She was smart enough to keep her bag tucked under her arm and cross the lot at a brisk pace. She was smart enough to be aware of the people around her—the couple making out beside a sports car, the group of college-age boys and their appreciative whistles and catcalls.

The lone figure creeping through the shadows behind her. Keeping pace, but staying just out of sight.

She battled the twinge of unease that rippled down her spine by lengthening her stride. Her car was only a row away now. Her keys were in one hand, her pepper spray in the other.

If she could just see a face. Identify him. It had to be a him. The breeze off the river chased her with the earthy stink of the water and the oily scent of the warm asphalt. But her nose detected something sweeter from the shadows. Too pungent to be a perfume. Cigar smoke? A pipe?

The lights from the casino had dimmed to a glow in the sky behind her. But she'd parked directly under a lamppost. She'd be safe in the light. She rounded the bumper of an SUV and headed straight for the glimpse of cherry-red five cars away.

The shadow continued straight on.

Rebecca breathed a sigh of relief. With cameras and bouncers and bosses with grabby hands, she was just being paranoid. Creating danger where none existed. She was alone out here. She was safe.

She had her key ready to unlock the door when she reached her car.

Rebecca froze. Gaped. Her bravado wilted.

"Oh. My. God."

Chapter Six

Don't mess with things that don't concern you.

The message scrawled across her windshield in thick, red paint was as clear and vile as the word carved into the hood.

B-I-T-C-H

In an act of pure, hate-fueled violence, her Mustang had been vandalized. Keyed. Dented. A tire had been slashed, a side mirror destroyed.

"My car." A gift from her father. Perfectly preserved the way he'd taught her. A girl on her own needed to know how to maintain a car, he'd always said, from the upholstery inside to the oil beneath the hood.

All her hard work, her tribute to her father, had been violated.

Ruined.

It felt like losing her father all over again.

"Oh, no." But Reuben Page had instilled some practicality into his girl. Pushing aside the sting of sentimental tears, Rebecca dashed around to the passenger side and unlocked the door. The exterior of her car could be repaired, ignored. But she'd hidden the real treasure inside.

The Go Away! written on the window smeared beneath her fingers. She paused a moment to rub the waxy substance between her thumb and fingertips, then sniff to identify it. Not paint at all. A color she could trace even without a crime lab. "Lipstick. Who would…?"

She shook off her speculation and swung open the door, diving inside to check the glove compartment. It was still there. "Thank God. Thank God."

At least one part of her father's memory hadn't been damaged. Rebecca wiped the makeup off on her pant leg and opened the glove box. She pulled out the worn leather notebook that connected her to his last night on earth and hugged it to her chest. "It's okay, Dad. It's okay."

She forced herself to breathe. In and out.

She forced herself to analyze what this meant. She'd really pissed someone off—come a little too close to a secret. Her questions had someone worried about what she could—and would—do next.

But victory was a fleeting thing.

Something moved in the shadows beyond the circle of lamplight. In the next row of cars. A shape, darker than the darkness around it. Still. Watching.

Curious bystander? Or something much more personal?

Rebecca slipped her father's notebook into her shoulder bag and climbed out of the car. She squinted, trying to bring the ominous shape into focus.

Was it the same man she'd thought had followed her before? Was it even a man? Was she still standing here? By herself? Letting that hateful presence see how this vile message had spooked her?

She was smarter than that. Reuben had raised her to be smarter than that.

When the shadow didn't move, Rebecca quietly closed the door and backed away. She circled the trunk of the car, keeping the figure in sight. She glanced around, making sure her path was clear, and kept backing up.

"Ace Longbow?" He'd waited in the shadows and watched her before. "You stay away from me. You stay away!"

With that bold shout, she spun around and ran toward the lights and people of the casino.

Were those footsteps? Breaking into a run? Following her?

Rebecca's heart pounded in her chest. The crunch of leather shoes on asphalt got louder.

She clutched her bag, lowered her head, rounded the SUV at the end of the row and ran smack into something warm and solid. Some*one* warm and solid.

Rebecca shoved. Screamed.

Strong hands latched onto her arms and trapped her. "Rebecca? Rebecca!"

With a firm shake, the gruff voice registered. The square face took shape and expression. The strong chest rising and falling beneath her hands was no shadow.

"Seth?" For one crazy moment, Rebecca wanted to throw her arms around his neck and cling to what seemed like the safest place on the planet. But a saner thought overrode that needy emotion. He was as much her enemy as the man in the shadows. Right? She wriggled in his grasp and tried to push his hands away. "What the hell are you doing, scaring me like that?"

"What's with the hundred-yard dash?"

"Was that you running after me?"

"Running *toward* you." He squeezed her shoulders, stilling her struggles with his insistent touch and the intense scrutiny of those gray-green eyes. "I heard you shouting at Ace." He looked beyond her, quickly scanned their surroundings. "Is he here?" His survey stopped at the red stain on her thigh and he swore. "Are you hurt?"

"What? No, it's just lipstick." Her skin burned beneath the denim when he touched her. His probing fingers were sure, precise. "Seth! I'm okay." She needed him to stop touching her so she could think. So she could stay sharp and fired up. She finally twisted free and clutched her bag like a shield between them. "What kind of security are you running at this place, anyway? What are you doing out here?"

"I was running a routine monitor sweep. But someone's disabled the parking-lot cameras. I thought I'd better check it out. Then I heard you shouting at Ace."

"Well, I know why the cameras aren't working." She led him to her car and pointed. "So some... coward...could do this."

"Son of a..." He circled the Mustang, reading every word, his expression growing more grim with every step. "Any idea who'd want to send you a message like this?"

"No, but I'm guessing it was a female. Even your deductive skills should be able to piece that together with the lipstick!"

Seth offered no argument, no words of false comfort or reassurance. But he took pictures with his cellphone, assessed each attack on her car, checked the neighboring vehicles and immediate area—moving from task to task as if this kind of work was routine—as if he owned the place. His take-charge sense of purpose made Rebecca feel a little less alone, a little less victimized. With Seth Cartwright inspecting them, the shadows seemed less of a threat.

As her anger at the attack diminished, other emotions—ones she was far less equipped to deal with—began to surface. "My dad gave me this Mustang. When I went off to college. It was his back when he was in school."

"I'm sure he'll just be glad you weren't hurt." Seth pulled his attention back from the parking lot around them. "Everything here can be fixed."

She hugged her bag tighter to her chest and clutched Reuben's ring in her fist, trying to dispel the chill that came from deep inside. "But I don't have that many things left from him."

"You dad's gone?"

"Yes! He…" She snapped her mouth shut once she realized she was revealing far too much.

When he saw she was done explaining the past, Seth switched back to the present. He guided her to the rear of the car where the damage was less evident. "Why do you think Ace did this?"

He was talking like a cop, acting like a cop. Rebecca bristled at the realization that right now she'd be pretty damn glad if he was still a cop. But she didn't like cops. KCPD gave up on her father's murder. They were the last place she should be turning to for answers and help.

"Bec?"

"Rebecca," she corrected absently, still sorting her thoughts.

He ignored her and moved closer. "Why Ace?"

"Because he was… Last night…"

"Ace was *what* last night?"

When Seth was right there—in her face, nose to nose—she couldn't look away. Or lie. "He was watching me. I was hiding on the deck, waiting for Teddy to leave in his limo—trying to avoid another run-in with you. I didn't know it at first, not until he lit a cigarette, but he was there, behind me. The whole time. Just…watching." She shivered. When Seth's hands folded around her bare arms and started moving up and down, sharing his warmth, she forgot to protest. "It creeped me out."

"Did he say anything?"

"Something about my luck running out. And then he bumped me."

The massage stopped. "He touched you?"

Rebecca shrugged. "I think he was mad about something else. He doesn't know who I really am."

"Ace lives in a perpetual bad mood. But that's no excuse for bullying you." She missed his warmth when his hands left her to pull out his cell phone and punch in a number. Someone picked up. "Yeah, this is Cart-wright."

"Who are you calling?"

"KCPD."

Real cops? She snagged his wrist and pulled the phone from his ear. "No, don't. Please."

"It's cool," he spoke into the phone, never taking his eyes off hers. "I'll talk to you later." He snapped the phone shut and clipped it back onto his belt. "Okay, so you're going to complain about my security, but you won't let me do my job?"

"I thought you were on the outs with them." If they checked out her car, then they'd be checking out what she was doing here. And KCPD didn't like reporters—especially her—figuring out the answers to crimes before they did. "I'll call it in."

"When?" His doubt was clear.

Rebecca backed away. He could read her too well when they were this close. But she was oddly reluctant to walk too far on her own. There. Between those two cars. Rebecca shivered. That's where the man had been. It was all a monochromatic haze now. The shadow was gone.

But with her back to the Mustang and the pain of seeing her father's legacy trashed behind her, her reporter's eye—and nose—for observation finally rebooted.

"Do you smoke?"

He walked up beside her, giving her a good whiff of clean soap and musky skin and nothing else. "No. Why?"

Maybe she was crazy, or maybe it was an important clue. "It's a nasty habit. Whether you're actually lighting up or not, the scent stays with you."

"Bec. What about the smoke?" He stood beside her, peering at the same spot now. "What else?"

"I thought I saw someone following me in the parking lot tonight. When I first heard you, I got you mixed up with him." She pointed between the parked cars. "But now I'm sure. There was someone. Right over there."

"You *thought* you saw?"

"I smelled him, actually. Smoke from the shadows beyond the lamp posts. Like a fancy cigar or cigarette." She shook her head, frustrated by her inability to fit the facts together. "Whatever I saw, though, it was too big to be a woman. And a guy wouldn't carry a lipstick. It was probably some sick curiosity seeker who stopped to watch me freak out while he had his cigarette."

"A woman can change her shape easily, just by putting on a coat. Or there could be accomplices."

"Or they could be unrelated events. I get the idea. You think I'm turning nothing into something."

"I didn't say that. Don't go looking for a fight when there's none to be had." She jumped when he wrapped his hand around hers. "Show me exactly where you saw this guy. We'll check the place for cigarette butts. Especially ones with lipstick marks."

Her immediate tensing eased as he held on, and Seth's touch infused her with a warmth that flowed up her arm and seemed to calm that defensive, independent place inside her. "Are you sure you're not a cop?"

"Some habits never die." He tugged. She fell into

step beside him. "C'mon. We'll check this out. Then I'll walk you inside. We'll make a couple of phone calls to KCPD and a garage, and then I'm driving you home."

"I can call a cab."

"This is too personal. I want to check out your place before I let you walk in by yourself."

"I've been on my own a long time, Cartwright. I know the rules. I'll check the locks before I go in. I'll have the super walk me up—"

"I'm driving you home."

He stated it as fact. She should have argued against his presumption.

She should have wanted to.

Instead, when he altered his grip to lace his fingers through hers, Rebecca took note of how well their hands fit together. And she held on. To Seth. To safety.

"Fine. You call the garage. I'll call the cops. Satisfied?"

"For now. We can use my office."

He tugged. She followed, sensing that she'd be spending the entire night in Seth's office if she didn't make that call. She couldn't legally report the crime under her assumed name, but she wasn't about to give KCPD her real name and alert them to the fact she was investigating a story at the Riverboat. Maybe she could call time and temp, or her own answering machine, and fake the conversation well enough for Seth to give it a rest. She'd work out the details of the charade later. For now, she was more willing than she should have been to stick to Seth's side as they crossed the parking lot.

The fact that Seth Cartwright seemed as concerned

about the vandalism as she was only made her take the warning that much more seriously. The fact that he had just appointed himself as some sort of personal body-guard for the night meant she'd have to be on guard against her words and actions now more than ever. It meant she'd have to guard her feelings as well. Because, for three long years, she hadn't allowed herself to depend on anyone. Especially not a cop. Not even an ex-cop.

But tonight she held tightly to Seth's hand.

REBECCA PAGE'S brownstone building off Walnut Street in downtown Kansas City had pretty decent security. Double front doors in the lobby. A security code. And, like any smart woman living on her own in the city, she had three separate locks on her apartment door. But none of it would stop Ace Longbow if he was determined to get to her.

"First you drive me home. Then you walk me up to the third floor. Now you're inspecting my bedroom." Rebecca stood in the doorway, her arms crossed in that perpetually defensive mode. Her mouth on the of-fensive again. Tonight Seth had learned that the sassy attitude was as much a cover for her emotions as the don't-give-a-damn chip on his shoulder was for him. But he'd felt the goose bumps on her skin tonight. He'd seen the terrified look in her eyes when she'd run smack dab into the middle of his chest at the Riverboat parking lot. "Just what is it you expect to find here, Cartwright?"

That she had clean, spartan taste in home decorat-ing, and a penchant for collecting stuffed animals that rivaled his sister's middle-school years. Who needed pictures or knick-knacks when you could line an entire wall three-feet deep with teddy bears, dogs and furry dragons? The dragon part he got, but he wouldn't have expected Rebecca to be the fuzzy, snuggly type.

Of course, he'd never expected to feel this tenuous unspoken connection to Rebecca Page, either. Their minds worked the same way—always suspicious, always observing. Their hearts seemed to work the same way, too—caring about the oddest things at the most inconvenient times. Like the abuse of a mutual friend, the senseless assault on a cherry-red Mustang or a haphazard pile of plush toys in an otherwise tidy apartment.

"Just because a man can't get through your front door doesn't mean he can't get to you." Seth took note of the red message light blinking on the answering machine beside her bed before assuring himself that the window in here was secure. He ushered her back into the living room ahead of him, passed her desk and the temptation of booting up her laptop to find out exactly what she was working on—and crossed straight to the double-hung windows there to make his point. "Any-one could come straight up this fire escape if he wanted to."

"Is that supposed to reassure me?"

He pulled back the front edges of his jacket and splayed his fingers at his waist. "It should remind you that you're vulnerable. You may have a good eye for watching what's going on around you at work, but most folks let down their guard when they get around the comforts of home."

She walked to the window and gestured to the darkened street below them. "C'mon, Cartwright. A guy would have to be over seven feet tall to jump up to the bottom of that fire escape and unhook the ladder."

Had she *seen* the size of Ace Longbow? But more important, he wanted to point out that determination and intent were bigger factors than the height of a man. "I could do it."

There it was. That slight hitch in her bravado. Next, the goose bumps would pop up across that smooth, velvety expanse of skin along her arms. Then she'd hug herself, tilt her chin, and pretend that the Amazon princess couldn't be rattled.

She was hugging herself when she turned to face him, and Seth debated whether he should grin victoriously at his ability to read her—or take her in his arms and offer some kind of comfort after spooking her with the truth. "Well, since I know you won't be climbing up to my window to play Romeo anytime soon, I won't worry about it."

He wisely slid his hands into his pockets and headed for the front door. He and Rebecca mixed like fire and ice. She wasn't interested in TLC from him and he wasn't interested in playing her games. She'd only stuck to his side in the Riverboat parking lot because he wore a gun and a title that offered her some degree of security. She'd have ditched him if some crazy hadn't trashed her car and then had the nerve to follow her to see her reaction to the threats. Or worse.

It was the *or worse* that had him searching for cigarette butts and insisting on checking Rebecca's home security set-up. He had certain duties he was expected to perform, such as seeing to the safety of the River-boat's employees. As a cop who couldn't entirely forget his conscience, no matter what undercover work demanded of him, he expected it of himself to see to the protection of anyone in danger.

He was here because the casino's surveillance cameras had been tampered with—probably to mask the attack on her car. He was here because whoever had gone to that much trouble to intimidate Rebecca had just moved up a notch on his most-wanted list at Wolfe International.

This had nothing to do with tender feelings he hadn't felt in months, or the way Rebecca Page's responsive skin and golden eyes screwed with his hormones.

No way. He couldn't afford to be playing Romeo with any woman right now.

"Yeah, well you're not exactly my idea of a Juliet."

"Too tall?" The verbal duel followed right behind him. "Too smart? Too much on the right side of the law?"

Seth spun around, planted his feet and forced that sassy bravado to back off a step.

"Do you have any idea of what's goin' on around you?" Sable curls bounced around her neck as she pulled up short. "Do you have any idea of the people you're messin' with?"

The chin tilted. She was going to bluff her way past admitting she felt any kind of vulnerability. "Ooh. You are a big bad tough guy, aren't you. If you're trying to scare me into thinking someone's going to break into my apartment so I'll quit the Riverboat and my story, you've got another think coming. You don't scare me, Cartwright."

He reached out and wound his finger inside a dark corkscrew of hair that had fallen over one shoulder. Cripes. It was as thick and silky as it looked. But if she could resolutely stand there and pretend she wasn't off her game tonight, then so could he. "I think I do."

"The truth isn't always convenient for you, is it?"

Seth pulled his finger free and watched the curl spring back against her neck. He traced his finger along the graceful arc of her collarbone, gently brushing the ribbons of hair behind her back. "Did you ever wonder why you and I fight all the time? Even when we have the same goals?"

"I never gave it that much…thought." Though she covered it by clearing her throat, the husky catch of her voice skittered across his skin. "Apparently, you have."

His gaze dropped to those full, unadorned lips. Oh yeah, he was definitely thinking about it now. "They say opposites attract. But that's not us. When two things are alike, they push against each other, create energy between them."

There was something pulsing deep inside him even now.

"I've heard better lines than that one. Are you trying to be a poet or a scientist?"

The tip of her tongue darted out to moisten her lips and that pulse became a pounding beat in his veins. He ought to get this urge to taste her out of his system, get his face smacked and get over it. Then he could go back to life as usual on this assignment.

Dangerous? To be expected. Lonely? He could deal with it. Predictable? Not exactly. But at least he knew who the players were, and over the past few months, he'd learned how Teddy or Ace or any of the others would react in a given situation. But Rebecca Page was a kink in the works. And reactions to her, thus far— especially his own—had been entirely *un*predictable.

"Definitely scientist. There's chemistry between us." His own voice sank deep into a throaty rumble as his fingers tangled in her ponytail and he drifted closer. "And that's what scares you. It's not that I'm a cop, or that my mom's the commissioner, or that KCPD wants you to go through the public information officer like every other reporter to get your story. That's not what gets you so riled up. It's that damned chemistry. We just keep pushin.' And it's drivin' you nuts that you can't control it."

He didn't hear the slip-up, but she did.

"Did you just admit you were a cop? You're not on probation, are you."

And then she pushed too hard.

Seth's breath rushed out on a frustrated sigh. He untangled his fingers from her hair, pulled back and shook his head. "You're a real piece of work."

"What are you doing at the Riverboat? What are you working on?"

"Ever the reporter, eh, *Poochman?*" he emphasized, nodding toward the computer and files on her desk, reminding her that secrets and lies went both ways. He spouted the story that had gotten him from the Fourth Precinct detectives division to the vice squad to trusted enforcer of Kansas City's number-one organized crime suspect. "I'm on probation from KCPD. And since they don't intend to pay me until Internal Affairs is done investigating me, I had to find myself another way to make some money. Austin introduced me to people at the Riverboat who could use my particular skills, and voilà."

"I don't buy that. I knew there was something up with you. Are you investigating Teddy Wolfe? What do you think he's up to? Do you have proof yet?"

His gaze went back to the framed photograph of her and an older man on her desk. An older man whose tall, lanky frame bore a familiar resemblance to the dark-haired siren standing before him now. Time for a diversion. "Who's that in the picture?" He took half a step around her and touched the picture frame. "Must be somebody pretty special since it's the only photograph in the whole apartment." He picked it up. "Is this your dad?"

"Hey, some of us actually have to work for a living and would like to get some sleep." Rebecca pried the picture from his grip and set it face-down on the desk. In the same fluid movement, she flattened her hand at the center of his chest and backed him up a step, wedging herself between him and the photograph. "I appreciate you being all gallant and seeing to my safety, Cartwright, but I'm a big girl. I can take care of myself."

Interesting. He'd hardly call this change in topic any more subtle than his had been. He let her push him toward the door. "So you're not inviting me to stay for coffee? I'd love to learn more about you. And your family. Seeing as how you've already met and persecuted all of mine. Don't you think that's fair?"

He knew how to press for information, too.

"I see what you mean about that push thing, Cartwright." His shoulder blades bumped the door and she drifted a hair's-breadth closer. Heat blossomed at his sternum beneath the press of her hand. She kept moving forward. "And just for the record? I'm not scared of you one damn bit."

Though he felt the heat of her body long before her thighs brushed against his, Seth wasn't prepared for the leaping response of every cell inside him when Rebecca's lips touched his own. There was no hesitancy in her bold approach. Her mouth was as soft and full and delicious as any fantasy he'd concocted thus far. She curled her fingers into a fist, grabbing up a handful of his shirt to hold him close while she ran her tongue along the seam of his lips and commanded them to open. When he obliged, her pliant mouth switched positions, experimenting to find the best fit before her sweet tongue darted inside to slide against his own.

For a moment, Seth simply let his hands rest at her hips and held on while she had her way with him. His pulse was humming, his skin was burning, and south of his belt buckle the pressure was surging at a healthy rate.

Damn fine diversion.

But two could play that game.

Seth tightened his grip at the swell of her hips and turned her, backing her against the wall to finish what she had started.

He covered her startled gasp with the demand of his mouth. At the soft moan of surrender in her throat, he pulled her hand from his shirt and looped her arms around his neck, removing that impediment so he could walk right into her body. The tips of her small breasts rubbed against his harder chest and tightened to proud peaks. Seth wound one arm behind her back and pulled them together, stomach to stomach, hip to hip, thigh to thigh. Her body was lean and strong, her lips feminine and perfect, and that hair... Seth freed her ponytail from its band and filled his palm with a handful of soft, kinky curls.

And, all the while, Rebecca held on, rubbing her fingers across the short hair at his nape and matching his demands on her. With every touch on her hair, the exotic spice of the shampoo she used teased his nose. With every deepening kiss, the fresh, sweet taste of her filled his mouth.

If the initial kiss was hot, then this full-body press had erupted into incendiary.

Somewhere in the back of his mind, he knew this was all a ploy. But he couldn't seem to help things getting out of hand. Months of playing verbal games and testing wills—as he protected his family from the press and Rebecca pushed and probed for her stories—had built up into a combustible tension that was finally being released.

But the crazy, damnable thing was that kissing Rebecca like this wasn't getting her *out* of his system. Touching her, tasting her, giving in to her was only stoking a need inside him to want more of her. All of her.

His hand was inside the back of her shirt, discovering there was no bra strap to obstruct his exploration before sensibility made a valiant effort to return. Skin to skin, he learned every inch of her was soft to the touch. Every inch of her was warm. Sexy. Responsive. Delicate. Feminine.

Hit the brakes, Cartwright.

He was supposed to be the guy in charge here. The one protecting her. The one who had to always stay one step ahead of her so she wouldn't bring down his entire investigation by pursuing her story.

Dragging his mouth from hers, pulling his hand from her skin and hair and adjusting her shirt to a more modest level, Seth forced a cooling whisper of common sense between them. He pulled her arms from around his neck and caught her wrists against the deep, ragged rise and fall of his chest.

The Amazon princess was breathing just as hard. The hazy expression in her tawny eyes revealed just as much surprise and confusion as he was feeling. Her hair was a wild, sensuous mess. Her tender, pinkened lips reminded him that they had been equal partners in passion.

And the sass from those lips—though a little breathless—was still firmly in place. "See? You can't scare me."

He touched a fingertip to the defiant tilt of her chin and grinned. He had her number. "Is that what we proved?"

She pushed against his chest. "Goodnight, Cartwright."

He rested his forehead against hers for a brief moment before pressing a chaste kiss to that same spot and pulling away entirely. "Goodnight, Bec."

"Rebecca," she corrected, just to make a point.

While he adjusted his sleeves, shirtfront and holster back into place, Rebecca unlocked the door and opened it. In the hallway, Seth paused to look back. Rebecca Page was a strong woman, with a lot of tough talk. But seeing her standing tall and proud in the doorway—freshly kissed, her breasts undeniably aroused beneath her shirt—he was struck by the notion that she was uniquely feminine and unexpectedly vulnerable beneath the surface. He also sensed that she was alone in the world—maybe even more alone than he.

Reasons enough to look out for her. Reasons enough to be on guard against the terrible tenderness taking root inside him that could only distract him from the dangers at the Riverboat and his ability to keep her safe. "Once I hear the dead bolt lock behind me I'll leave."

Minutes later, Seth was making himself at home behind the wheel of his truck, waiting for the lights to go out in Rebecca's third-floor apartment. Meanwhile, he pulled out his cell phone and punched in Cooper Bellamy's number. Over the past several months his partner had gotten used to odd phone calls like this one at three in the morning.

Curious that he didn't wake him up, though. Coop picked up on the first ring. "Hey, what was going on earlier when you hung up on me?"

"Worried about me?" Seth teased, shifting to a more comfortable position to let the frustrated desire still lingering from that kiss ease from his body.

"Always. Answer the question."

"I think tensions at the Riverboat just escalated a notch. Either I'm about to get everything I need to put Wolfe and his men away for good—or it's all gonna blow up in my face."

"I vote for option one if you don't mind."

"Me, too."

"So what changed?"

"I've got an extra party throwing a catalyst into the mix. Setting tempers on edge, moving some of our players into action."

"*Extra party* as in Rebecca Page?"

"Don't sound so curious, you big goof ball. Nothing happened." It was a lie. Coop probably knew it, but could read Seth's moods well enough not to push it. "You at home or work?"

Coop laughed. "I'm slaving away, night and day, to protect your ass. I went down to the station house as soon as you called earlier because I didn't know what you'd need and I wanted to be prepared for anything. What's up?"

"You have access to a KCPD computer?"

"Sure. Right here on my desk."

"I want you to look up tonight's logs and see if Rebecca filed a vandalism report on her car. Look up *Poochman* as well as *Page*."

"I'm checking. What happened?" Seth gave his partner a thumbnail account of tonight's events, from the sabotaged parking-lot cameras to the crude message on Rebecca's car to the possibility that someone was following her. Since Coop didn't need any fodder to give him a hard time, he left out any mention of that steamy kiss. "Hell. She doesn't do anything in a small way, does she?"

Rebecca's effect on Seth wasn't small, either.

It didn't take long to give Coop the details. It didn't take his partner long to find an answer, either.

"There's nothing here. Under either name."

Seth swore. Crazy woman. What was she really after?

"I didn't think there would be." She must have called a fake number from his office, probably her own answering machine. "How soon can you get me that background check on her?"

"I'm puttin' it together now. Let's set up a time and place to meet."

"Make it later tonight. I'm gonna need some sleep. Hey, find out who her father is, while you're at it. Or who he *was*. I think it's important."

"Will do."

They made the arrangements and hung up. Seth placed the phone beside him on the seat, pulled his gun into his lap for immediate access and settled in to catch a cat nap. Rebecca Page was apparently as much of a night owl as he was.

That woman was playing with fire.

And Seth had an unsettling feeling they were both going to be irrevocably burned.

Chapter Seven

"Wow." Rebecca trailed her fingers along the damp, faintly slimy chill of the old pipes that honeycombed one wall of the *Commodore*'s engine room. She wiped her hand on the leg of her jeans and raised her lantern up to the silver-haired gentleman beside her. "It looks like everything has been frozen in time down here."

"As rusted out as the hull was getting, most of the compartments below deck are surprisingly well-preserved." Austin Cartwright was proving to be an invaluable source of information.

Neither of them made mention of the night before when Teddy had practically thrown Austin out of the casino for making a scene. He was probably embarrassed at being called down by the casino's owner, and that rescuing his daughter from Teddy's flirtations was the only thing that had finally gotten him away from the tables.

And Rebecca certainly didn't want to revisit the way last night had ended for her. Beyond the extremely personalized impact of the messages on her father's car, kissing Seth Cartwright might not have been the smartest move on her part. That push-push attraction he'd gone on about made an embarrassing amount of sense. Because somewhere in the middle of that kiss, the power between them had shifted. The magnetic poles that kept them apart had flipped, and for several long, agonizingly hot moments, she couldn't get close enough to him. She'd forgotten her purpose in kissing him, forgotten who she was, forgotten everything but the way he made her feel alive and sexy and hopeful in his arms.

Sure, she'd diverted his interest away from that photo of her father. But he'd left her to doze on and off through the remainder of the night with fitful dreams, ranging everywhere from Seth simply holding her hand and making her feel as though he could keep the shadows at bay—to stripping their clothes off and finding out whether those insistent hands of his could make her feel as feverishly female on other parts of her body as they had on her back and in her hair.

And though she wanted to ask Austin why he and Seth rarely spoke, and whether or not his tough-guy son had learned his chivalrous determination to walk her to her front door from his father or his mother, they'd silently agreed that, like gambling, the River-boat's Chief of Security was a taboo subject.

As long as they stuck to history, Rebecca found that she and Austin had a lot to talk about. Not only had he brought out the ship's original blueprints for her to study, but he'd taken her down into the internal workings of the *Commodore* itself—inviting her to walk in the very footsteps her father must have left behind in the final moments before his death up on the *Commodore*'s deck.

"It was my intention from the very beginning of the project to keep the casino's design as historically accurate as possible." Austin brushed away the cobwebs that had caught on the upright handle of the engine's rpm-control stick. "It took a great deal of persuasion to convince Wolfe International that going back to the 1938 design would create something unique, would draw in tourists as well as the usual gambling clientele. Personally, I feel the ghosts of the *Commodore* are as big a draw as the craps tables upstairs."

"Ghosts?" There was only one ghost she was interested in. But she had a feeling Austin was speaking figuratively, not literally.

He swung the beam of his flashlight into the shadowed nooks and crannies of the long, low-ceilinged room. "The stories this old girl could tell. Honeymoon trips. Charter cruises by the likes of movie stars and millionaires. Rumor has it that then vice-president Truman and his wife, Bess, rode it all the way to St. Louis and on down to New Orleans, stumping for war bonds during the Second World War."

"I heard that bootleggers used the hold to smuggle homemade hooch and other black-market items during the war." Though Rebecca was busy memorizing the layout of the ship's lower decks and noting that there were no security cameras down here, she thought it wise to ask a question or two for her supposed story. Even if Austin's zealously distrustful son doubted her excuse for being here, she still had the rest of her co-workers believing in her cover. "Is that true?"

"Anything's possible." Austin stroked his hand

across the control console. "She was designed by a woman. That probably raised a few eyebrows back in the day. Now she's been left in my trusted care."

"You mean Wolfe International's," Rebecca clarified.

Austin bristled at the correction. "I have a stake in the ownership of this casino, so it's mine as much as anybody's. I traded my design expertise for shares in the company."

"I heard there were some problems getting the whole renovation project off the ground. That the city's Economic Development Committee didn't want another casino." She was fishing for information. Evidence of a bribe or intimidation would provide a motive for killing her father.

But Austin didn't take the bait. "Once Teddy Wolfe came on board with his money, the committee green-lighted the project. He had the cash. Kelleher had the connections. And I had the vision."

So which one of them had eliminated the one man standing in the way of their success?

But since that was the one question she couldn't ask, Rebecca tried a different tack. "Is that what Teddy meant last night when he said you owed him? He made the Riverboat happen for you and Kelleher?"

Austin's face turned ashy beneath his salon tan. "I suppose I should be grateful that Teddy hired me to do the renovation when no one else would give me the time of day. But if anything, Teddy owes me."

"What?" She turned away to keep the anticipation of finding an answer from showing on her face. "What did you do for Teddy?"

"That's business." Subject closed. Answer denied. "If you'd like to see more of the ship, we'd better get going before you have to report to work."

Disappointed as she was in failing to discover what favor Austin had done for Teddy Wolfe, Rebecca turned her attention back to the ship. There were answers to be found here, too, if she could just decipher them. "I'd like to just stay here and look around for a while if that's okay."

"Of course. If you have any questions, ask away."

The sketch she'd memorized from her father's dead hand had an arrow pointing down from the letters *COM. Commodore.* Even with the new facades and modernizations, it was easy to figure out that he'd wanted her to go down inside the ship. *I'm here, Dad.* With company beside her, she kept her thoughts to herself. *What do you want me to find?*

Austin pulled out a thin but neatly-ironed handkerchief and began polishing the glass casing over the engine's speed and directional console. Bit by bit, red enamel letters—still bright despite their age—took shape.

Bit by bit, another piece of the puzzle Reuben Page had left behind began to fall into place.

The control console.

One last sweep through the dust revealed the words *Ahead Full.* Rebecca curled her toes inside her tennis shoes to check the keen sense of discovery that made her want to run to Austin's side. AF A1/2 AS had meant nothing to the detectives who'd read the scribbles on her father's palm. But she now recognized the clues for what they were—*Ahead Full. Ahead Half. All*

Stop. Not markings of a ship's speed, but a signpost guiding her through the engine room to where he'd hidden a clue to his murder.

He was showing her the way.

She hoped.

"Does that still work?" Rebecca carefully stepped over a steel floor joist and gripped the handle. A thrust forward sent a shower of chipped white paint to the floor. A good tug pulled it back to the All Stop marking. AS. Underlined twice. An arrow pointing her toward…

Rebecca tilted her chin. She squeezed the muscles of her face to keep from breaking out with a triumphant grin. Above the All Stop position were two rectangular steel doors. Each hatch had its own, wheel-shaped locking mechanism to seal it shut.

The answers to her father's murder could be hidden inside.

Looping the strap of her flashlight over her wrist, Rebecca gripped the lower wheel in her fists and tried to turn it. She pushed and pulled. Her arms shook with the pressure she exerted, but the damn thing wouldn't budge.

She swallowed an unladylike curse and grunted her frustration.

"Curious one, aren't you?" For a split second, she'd forgotten she had company. But instead of questioning her rabid fascination, Austin placed his hands on the wheel on either side of hers and counted to three. "Time and humidity have swelled and rusted nearly everything below decks. Here…" Was that a give? "We…" Metal screeched against metal. "Go."

"Yes!" The wheel ground away, spinning more easily with each rotation. "Will it open?"

The wheel stopped and Rebecca and Austin pulled. With a sucking pop, the compartment door swung open. The weight of the heavy metal scraped across its hinges. It couldn't be this easy, could it?

Rebecca turned her flashlight beam into the small black hole. Damn. Disappointment made her knees weak. As the adrenaline of hope waned, she grasped the side of the hatch to hold herself up on tiptoe. "Empty."

"Nasty." Austin stepped back and pulled out his handkerchief to wipe his hands.

There was nothing inside but some rat droppings and the musty stench of seventy years.

"When do you suppose was the last time anyone was in here?" Rebecca asked, already turning her attention to the sealed hatch above her and calculating whether her father, a tall man, would have been able to reach it.

"Before it was decommissioned in the sixties, I expect. So long as everything remained watertight, the new owners had no reason to come down here. They never had any intentions of firing up the engines and moving her."

"New owners? You mean Teddy?" She could open one hatch on her tour and chalk it up to curiosity. But she'd have to wait until she could come back alone— with a stepladder, perhaps—to open the upper compartment. However, if Austin Cartwright was willing to talk, she'd keep milking the source. "Is he the one who picked out Kansas City and the *Commodore* as an acquisition for Wolfe International?"

"Teddy? That boy doesn't have one original thought in his head. He'll be lucky if he doesn't throw away the entire fortune his father made in Europe. He wants to prove that he's his own man, but all he's proving is that he doesn't have the foresight to see beyond the length of his…" Austin's interest in discussing the past suddenly soured. He turned toward the steep metal stairs that led down into the engine room. "Ignore that rant. I'd better get you back upstairs. The evening shift starts in half an hour. Besides, I'd like to wash up before I hit the casino."

So there was no love lost between Austin and Teddy. That was an interesting enough tidbit that she wanted to follow up on the discord among the casino's major players. Maybe she could get one of them to turn on another and reveal what had happened to her father. But her well of information had dried up. For now. She'd resigned herself to the idea that there would be no quick and easy answers to Reuben's murder.

"Sure." A row of utility lights brightened the air as Rebecca climbed out into the access corridor. Using the excuse of helping the older man over the last step, she turned to memorize the engine room's exact location. "You're at the casino almost every night. This really is a hands-on, labor-of-love project for you, isn't it?"

She swallowed a protest as he pulled the access door shut and sealed it with a chain and padlock behind him. For safety reasons, he explained, even though Rebecca had silently hoped it wouldn't be necessary.

Was picking a lock as easy as it looked on television? Or did she have to be built like, well—Seth Cartwright—to handle a pair of bolt cutters?

"It's good business to mingle with the customers,"

Austin continued. "I can get a slow game moving, teach newbies how to play or place a bet. I like to be around the energy and possibilities there."

Possibilities? Rebecca climbed the next set of stairs ahead of her tour guide, wondering if she'd find someone else's stolen chips if she tried to pick his pocket for the key to the engine room. Over the last few days, she'd spent enough time with Austin to see that although he acted like a high-roller at the Riverboat, there was a worn look to his expensive suits and accessories. Either they were the same ones he'd had for years, or he'd bought them secondhand. Maybe what he owed Teddy was a boatload of money.

How sad that places like the Riverboat existed, tempting men with Austin's apparent weakness. It was unforgivable that people like the man who'd killed her father had no qualms about taking advantage of an illness such as Austin Cartwright's.

Is that what had created the obvious rift between Austin and Seth? Rebecca's bond with Reuben had been so tight, she couldn't imagine what it would be like to have her father around—working in the very same building—and yet have nothing to do with each other. Beyond perfunctory inquiries relating to casino business, she'd yet to see father and son share a personal conversation, much less trade a smile or handshake.

How sad.

How lonely.

On impulse—maybe because she missed her own father so much—Rebecca held out her hand as they reached the service corridor leading to the employees' locker rooms and casino entrance on the main deck. She smiled, leaned in and kissed his cheek. "Thanks, Austin. I appreciate the tour, as well as the answers to all my questions."

He folded both hands around hers and held on, blushing a little at the show of affection. "My pleasure. It's not often a pretty young thing like you—well, anyone—will listen to me go on about beams and bulkheads and historical integrity."

Her smile broadened. "I enjoyed it."

He nodded, hesitating a moment before breaking away and reaching into his pants pocket. He pulled out a shiny silver dollar and held it up between his thumb and forefinger.

Rebecca noted the larger size, and the eagle's wing beneath his finger. Definitely an antique. And probably worth far more than a single dollar. "Wow." She tried to sound appropriately impressed. "I haven't seen one of those for a long time."

"I've had it since I was a boy. It's my lucky dollar. I figure as long as I have this, I'll never truly go broke." His eyes sparkled as though he was that young boy again. "Would you rub it? I feel positive energy when I'm around you. I want to take that with me when I hit the tables."

Perhaps she hadn't fully realized the extent of his addiction until this moment. "Maybe you should have a coin collector appraise that," she suggested. "Or invest it. I'm sure either option would be a safer bet than losing it in the casino."

"Oh, I'll never get rid of this baby. Just touch it. I'm feeling lucky tonight."

As the *positive energy* in his expression took on that same tinge of madness she'd seen last night, Rebecca glanced up and down the deserted hallway. Her gaze alit on the security camera anchored to the ceiling beyond Austin's shoulder. It was foolish, really, wishing Seth was here to help her make the right choice, to help her say the right thing. Was he at the other end of that security feed? Watching her? Wishing she'd go away?

Maybe, for the first time, she could understand his ready mistrust of her as well.

A week ago, she had no reservations about using a man who'd stolen from her. But this moment spelled out in no uncertain terms that there were consequences for her deception. How could she care about this man's trouble, about Melissa's—about anyone and the problems they faced—without jeopardizing her investigation or compromising a story? Did she get tough with Austin and risk blowing the most useful relationship she'd developed at the Riverboat?

She touched her father's ring through the ribbing of her aqua tank top. But precious though it was, the band of gold couldn't offer any advice. The camera and the man who might or might not be watching certainly weren't going to. What the hell? She'd been alone for three years now and had learned to make her decisions all by herself. She'd make this one, too, and damn those consequences.

Rebecca wrapped her fingers around Austin's hand and the coin clutched inside. "I'll give you a dozen of these if you *don't* gamble tonight."

"Don't worry. I never bet this one."

"Don't bet anything. You can't build a fortune based on luck, Austin. You can't even pay your bills that way. You have a serious problem."

"I have an ex-wife and two children who give me that lecture every time I see them. I don't need to hear it from you, too."

"Maybe they tell you that because they care about you."

His face hardened, locking a smile that never reached his eyes into place. He'd rehearsed that fake indifference a hundred times. He pulled away and dropped the silver dollar back into his pocket. "Like I said, I'm feeling lucky. Don't jinx it by worrying about me." He tapped his watch, dismissing both her and her concern. "You don't want to be late for work. Wouldn't want to have to report you to the boss."

"Austin—"

"Stick to history, Rebecca." He winked and walked away before she could stop him with any other argument.

Great. Just great. So, in her effort to do justice by one father, she was letting another dad self-destruct without putting up a worthy fight. Rebecca nodded, rationalizing the guilt she felt. As soon as she found her father's murderer, she could turn her energy toward helping Austin. Unless Austin was somehow involved in Reuben's death. He had done Teddy some unknown *favor*. Then…

"Stop it," she chided herself. "It has to be done."

She hurried to the locker room to change for her shift at the Cotton Blossom. A good reporter stuck to the facts and didn't let her emotions get in the way of finding the story. Not with pushy security chiefs. Not with their fathers.

She wouldn't let emotional connections to new friends or father figures—or whatever the heck Seth Cartwright was to her—complicate her mission here. Time to shut down any guilt, compassion or need and get down to the job at hand.

Can't you take a hint, bitch?
We don't want you here, stirring up trouble.
I know what you're really after.
You'll never get it.
Go away.

REBECCA CRUMPLED the vile note in her hand. Written on the back of the same business card for a women's shelter she'd stuck in Melissa Teague's locker. It had fallen out of her own locker, from the folds of her ruffled collar, when she'd pulled out her dance-hall-girl costume to change for work. That seemed personal enough.

She didn't know whether to blow her stack or be scared spitless.

Half-dressed and clutching the hate mail inside her fist, Rebecca paced up and down each row of benches and lockers, looking for one knowing glance. One satisfied smile at her expense.

But everyone was busy pulling on hose and miniskirts, tying on bustles and primping hair. The person who'd left her the lovely missive was either long gone, or a damn fine actress.

Feeling frustrated, alone and properly terrorized,

Rebecca returned to her locker and sank onto the bench. She cradled her father's ring in her hand and prayed for insight. *I know what you're really after.* Who knew she was looking for Reuben's killer? Probably the killer himself. Where could she turn to for help without giving herself away?

Her editor? She was supposed to be on vacation. The police? *Hi, I'm conducting my own murder investigation. Is there any way you could protect me without having to arrest me for taking the law into my own hands?* Yeah, that'd go over real well.

What if she unwittingly turned right into the arms of the real killer?

She raised the ring to her lips and kissed it. "What do I do, Dad?" she whispered. "What do I do?"

He'd want her to know the truth.

So she flattened the card against her thigh and pulled Reuben's notebook from her tote bag. Chalk up one more clue that meant little out of context. She slipped the card between the pages. One day, it would all make sense. One day, she'd have more than a ring and a notebook and a beat-up car to honor her father's memory.

She'd have justice.

Instead of finishing getting changed, Rebecca opened Reuben's notebook and thumbed to the back pages. She made notations on the map there, marking camera positions and circling the engine room two decks below her. Dani Ballard's disk had to be there. If not, something she could use as hard evidence must be hidden inside the second compartment.

She was jotting her thoughts on Austin's gambling

addiction—and how Teddy could use that against him to force him to do whatever task he wanted—when a couple of the women at the front of the room squealed. Rebecca stopped with her pen poised over the open book. She heard a low-pitched voice, and a half-dozen protests before the click of heels and rustle of uniforms marked a general exodus out the door.

For one horrible moment she thought she'd been left alone with Ace. With that shadow. With someone she was more than certain she didn't want to be left alone with.

She was on her stocking feet to investigate when Dawn Kingsley popped her head around the corner of the last locker. Rebecca jumped.

"You've got company."

"Me?"

They'd given up on pleasantries since the first night Teddy had kissed her hand. And from her post at the front doors, Dawn had watched that whole hands-on pinchfest at the craps table last night. Was Teddy here?

Dawn sneered the instant Rebecca pulled on her striped top and started to button it. "No need to get dolled up. It's not who you want it to be."

Seth Cartwright's broad shoulders dwarfed the tiny blonde as he circled behind her and urged her toward the door. "Shoo."

Dawn's smirk barely registered before she disappeared.

The expectancy of getting closer to Teddy Wolfe instantly transformed into a different sort of anticipation. Rebecca's fingers froze at the second button. She tipped her chin, defying the edgy rush of awareness that quickened her pulse. She was prepping for the inevitable battle, she rationalized. Not another kiss. "What are you doing here?" she asked.

Seth didn't move until the door closed behind Dawn. "What's wrong?" he asked. With an easy alertness to his stride, he closed the distance between them, stopping with little more than her locker door between them. He closed his hands over her upper arms and started massaging, up and down. "And don't say 'nothing' because you're pale as a ghost and cool to the touch."

What was it with this guy and her personal space, anyway? And why was she twining her arms around his neck and closing what distance was left between them?

Rebecca rubbed her cheek against his rougher one and snuggled up to his strength and warmth.

"Okay" was all he said, moving the massage to her shoulders and back as he held her close. There was nothing to be said. It was just that feeling of security she craved. Seth's surprisingly tender comfort sparked a whole different set of nerve endings than that passionate kiss last night had. He smelled of man and confidence, and felt like a haven personified. But just as it had with that kiss last night, common sense kicked in. Rebecca gathered her thoughts and emotions and knew she had to retreat.

"Are you gonna talk, Poochman?"

She brushed the hair off her face and straightened his collar as she pulled away. She tried to blow off the knowledge that her fear hadn't truly abated until she'd seen his stern, chiseled face. Then it had rushed to the surface and evaporated beneath his steady, purposeful touch. "It was just a moment of weakness," she joked, turning back to her locker. "I'm over it." She snapped her fingers and frowned, needing to recapture that taunting banter that kept that familiar space between them. "Why are you in the women's dressing room, anyway?"

"There are no cameras in here," he explained matter-of-factly. "It's safe to talk."

"Oh." Made sense. Did not. "And you have something urgent to discuss?"

"I have some advice about Austin."

"So you *have* taken up voyeurism."

"I saw you two talking in the corridor. I'm trying to watch your back. But nobody else needs to hear this."

"How noble."

"I'm not here to pick a fight."

"That's a first." His gaze dropped to the open notebook, lying face down on the bench. A golden eyebrow arched in prelude to a query, but Rebecca quickly closed the book, dropped it into her tote bag and stuffed the whole thing into her locker. Right. Not suspicious. Not at all. "Oh, hell."

Resigned to the fact that Seth was too observant for *her* own good, Rebecca reached into her bag and pulled out the card. "This was in my locker this evening."

Seth read the note. He cursed like the cop he wasn't supposed to be anymore, stuffed the card inside his pocket with a promise to track down the writing somehow, and looked her in the eye. "And my chances of convincing you to give up this *history* research you're doing are…?"

"Nil."

"Rebecca—"

"Melissa needs me. You said so yourself. Your father needs me. I am not letting this coward chase me away."

"My father doesn't need anything."

"Seth!"

"I don't want you to feed his addiction!"

The green in his eyes warmed the gray away, leaving Rebecca with the oddest sensation that few people ever got to see him without the cool shroud of indifference he wore like a suit of armor.

She instantly regretted her defiance. Pulling her locker door halfway shut to mask her personal things, she faced him. He was serious. She could be, too. "He stole some chips from me the first night I was here, but I never mentioned it. Other than that, I haven't given him any money. In fact, I tried to talk him out of going to the casino tonight."

"Fat chance of that. Just make sure you keep your purse locked tight. And if he starts going on about his lucky silver dollar again, walk away. He may act like he cares about you, but don't trust anything he says. He takes advantage of the people closest to him. He can't help it."

Is that how Seth felt about his father? That Austin had betrayed his trust and taken advantage of him? "Seth—"

He nipped her curiosity in the bud by abruptly changing the topic. "Did you enjoy your tour of the ship?"

It was Rebecca's turn to bristle. Had he been tracking his father's movements or her own? "Austin loves to talk about the *Commodore*'s history. And I enjoy listening."

"Uh-huh."

"Maybe if you or someone he cares about encouraged him to pursue his other interests—like nautical history and architecture—it'd be easier for him to walk away from the casino and get the help he needs."

"You don't think we've tried that?"

"If you spent some time with him—"

"I spent sixteen years with him before he walked away. *He* left us. He chose his addiction over his family. My mother and sister and I have been where you are now, thinking you're gonna save him. You can't." He pushed the locker door shut the rest of the way, as though he wasn't already close enough for her to see the intent that deepened the angles of his face. "Saving Austin isn't why I'm letting you stay, anyway."

"Letting me—?" Rebecca huffed past her instinct to argue and tried to imagine the hurt and anger of a teenage boy whose father had chosen gambling over him. Seeing him now, it was hard to picture a younger, trusting version of Seth, with hope shining from his bold, masculine features. His issues with Austin had clearly carved some of the grooves that lined his firm mouth and colored his communication skills.

Almost without thinking, she reached out to touch the deep arc beside his mouth that became a dimple when he flashed one of those bemused grins. But heat leapt between them the instant she made contact, and she quickly curled her fingers into her palm and pulled back.

No kissing. No touching. Push. Push.

"I'm sorry. I was so close to my own dad that I can't imagine not wanting…" She stopped talking and took a moment to remind herself of her priorities. She shouldn't be discussing fathers with Seth. Seth couldn't find out that her being here had anything to do with Reuben. Cop or not, he'd have his own thoughts about tracking down a murderer. And they wouldn't include her. What words of comfort or reassurance could she say that he would listen to, anyway? "I'm sorry."

The green eyes shuttered to steely gray. "How's it going with Melissa?"

Apparently, the subject of fathers was closed. She should be breathing a sigh of relief, right?

Filing away the idea that Seth's emotions went far deeper than she'd given him credit for, Rebecca silently agreed to shift to a more neutral topic. "I took her to lunch today. Down on the Plaza."

The Plaza was an historic shopping and entertainment district south of downtown Kansas City. It was full of Mediterranean architecture, a variety of restaurants and specialty shops. And it was far away from the Riverboat.

"Did she have a good time?"

"Other than not feeling well, I think so. She says she has an ulcer, but we ate soup and sandwiches at one of the sidewalk cafés and bought a toy for her son. It was a nice break for both of us."

Seth pulled back the edges of his jacket and propped his hands at his hips, assuming a stance that passed for relaxed with Mr. Intensity. "Did she say anything?"

"Not about her boyfriend."

"He's an ex."

What? "If you know who's doing this to her, then why—?"

"I don't know if he's the one hurting her. It could have been a business-related assault."

No matter his claims to the contrary, *that* sounded like a cop talking.

But Rebecca was more interested in what he hadn't said. "What kind of business could a woman who talks about nothing but her kid and going back to college be involved with that could get her into that kind of trouble?"

"She's been at the Riverboat since it opened. She's been privy to a few things."

"Such as?" Frustrated with his mix of dire warnings and stringent lack of information, Rebecca pressed her palms against the nubby silk of his jacket and twisted her fingers into his lapel. She felt the strap of his holster underneath, felt his heat and his hardness—felt a scarily familiar need to pull him closer. Any one of those should have been enough to warn her off. But still she tugged, determined to shake some cooperation from the immovable object before her. "For once in your life, give me a straight, complete answer. What *business* are you talking about? Does it have anything to do with Teddy taking her out on the deck last night for a private conversation?"

"He thinks he's helping."

"Bull. Teddy's charm is all about manipulation. The only person he truly wants to help is himself."

Seth's hands settled at her waist, as if there was

nowhere else it made sense for them to go. "You picked up on that, huh?"

"Considering he always has Ace Longbow or Shaw McDonough lurking around him to keep away anyone he *doesn't* want to deal with, yeah, I think Teddy's intentions are pretty selfish."

"Were Ace or Shaw with him last night? Ganging up on Melissa?" Seth's grip tightened, demanding an answer.

"Not exactly— Ow!" Rebecca pulled on the elastic of her waistband to find out what hurt.

Seth instantly released her, putting his hands up in mock surrender as she twisted around to inspect the dark violet bruise on her hip. "Did I do that? Last night?"

Rebecca glanced over and saw something she never expected to see in Seth's eyes. Remorse.

He'd irritated her in a variety of ways any number of times. But he'd never physically hurt her. With his genuine concern over Melissa's injuries so evident, she hastened to reassure him. "Don't worry. It's Teddy's handiwork. Not yours."

"That son of a bitch."

"So much for employee loyalty." A shot of sarcasm eased some of the guilt from his expression. Turning the conversation back to *business* gave his face that familiar chiseled scowl once more. "We were discussing Melissa? Ace was there to make sure she and Teddy were alone out on the deck. But he wasn't part of their conversation."

Looking eminently relieved, Seth scraped his hand over his jaw and sank onto the bench between the rows of lockers. "You know, Melissa was actually crazy enough to be married to Ace once upon a time. Before I knew her."

Rebecca sat beside him. "No way."

"Way."

"That sweet thing and…him?"

Seth nodded. "He's her little boy's father. Though I don't think Ace has much to do with him."

"Restraining order?"

"He's just not interested in being a daddy. From what I understand, she was fresh out of high school when she got pregnant. I guess she thought she could change him. Save him. I don't think she knew what she was getting into."

Having a man in the women's locker room didn't seem quite so weird anymore, now that Seth was opening up and sharing information with her. She didn't want to spoil the opportunity by pushing too hard too fast. But she had to ask, "What was she getting into?"

"Trouble."

Rebecca schooled her patience at the annoyingly brief answer. "Did Ace abuse her when they were married?"

"I don't know. She doesn't talk about it. That's why I was hoping maybe you could get her to open up."

She hadn't had a lot of luck getting into anything deep with Melissa. But she was making a real friend. And it hurt to see her suffer. "Even if he never hit her, Melissa must have been terrified of Ace. I mean, I stand a head taller than she does, and with just a look he…"

Rebecca thought of the large, faceless shadow that

had followed her across the parking lot last night. It was all too easy to imagine Ace's cold black eyes filling that void. Watching her. Hating her.

She shivered at the idea of what might have happened if she'd been alone in that parking lot. Standing there in shock at the destruction of her father's beloved car. What if Seth hadn't been observant enough to know something was wrong?

"Hey." Seth's warm hand curled around her own, pulling her from the dark corners of her imagination. He laced his fingers through hers, pulling her hand into his lap and cradling it between both of his. "You get goose bumps like nobody's business when you get spooked."

He rubbed warmth into her hand, then swept his palm up and down her forearms, chasing away the chill. "The air conditioning is cranked too high in this place," she muttered.

But he didn't buy her weak excuse. And she didn't pull away from his gentle touch. "Has Ace done something else to you?"

He dipped his chin and Rebecca found herself looking straight into eyes that were warm and bright and real. How did she describe the threat she'd felt that first night at the Riverboat? The contempt she'd felt that day in the security office? Or last night in the bar? Why would she share that fear with Seth? Why did she think he'd understand?

"Bec?" Her name was a gruff rumble in his throat. "Talk to me. Has Ace done something? Did he hurt you? Did Teddy?"

Forcing her fears aside, Rebecca got her act together

and shrugged off his concern. "Other than somebody using my car to send me hate mail, and Teddy pinching the life out of me so he could keep his cool while he flirted with your sister last night, I'm fine."

"What?" Seth frowned. The massage stopped. "Flirting with Sarah?"

"Now who's asking all the questions?" she teased. He didn't laugh. "I thought you were watching me 24/7 on those security cameras. Didn't you see her come in last night to try to get your father away from the tables? Teddy went out of his way to introduce himself."

Seth swore. But she couldn't tell if his anger was over Teddy's treatment of his sister, his father or her. Maybe all three. "I was dealing with a woman who got her purse stolen. I didn't know. But no one got hurt?"

Rebecca gauged the sincerity in those dramatic, telling eyes and wondered how one man could make her feel so low and unwelcome with just a look, while this man made her feel safe and important with an equally intense gaze.

She shook her head of those completely feminine and completely irrelevant observations and pulled away. "Maybe your father's pride?" She stood and picked up her costume accessories. "Don't worry about your sister. She handled it all just fine. She was definitely more worried about your dad than about Teddy." He rose to block her path to the mirrors. "What?"

Seth fingered the gold chain that rested against her chest, lifting the ring she wore there. "You're always wearing this. Class of '77. Is it your boyfriend's?"

Realizing she was still half-exposed, still standing

within touching distance—still wanting him to touch
her—she snatched the ring back and turned away to
finish buttoning her costume. "Is that your subtle way
of asking me if I'm seeing anyone?"

"I'd ask you flat-out if I wanted to know." He waited
a beat, then asked, "Are you?"

His directness didn't surprise her. His interest did.
"No."

"I thought not. If a man cared about you, he
wouldn't let you be a part of this place."

Another warning. More questions with no
answers. His cryptic caveman routine was getting
old. "No man is going to tell me what I can and
cannot do."

Was that a laugh? A snicker, at least. The dimple
reappeared.

"I picked up on that." She must have imagined his
amusement. Because she saw nothing resembling a
smile when she turned to meet his gaze. "Don't get
involved with anyone while you're here. Not Teddy.
Not Ace. Not even my dad."

Did that list include him? "You can't just order me
to—"

"That's what got Melissa into trouble. Caring about
someone she shouldn't have." He freed a strand of hair
that had caught in her neckline and smoothed it behind
her shoulder. If they were two different people in a different place and different situation, she'd have thought
that was a caress. She'd have *wanted* it to be a caress.

"Finish your story and get out of here," he whispered. "Whatever it is. Don't let it get personal."

Too late, she wanted to answer, confused by the tender side of Seth Cartwright. *Too late.*

He patted the chest pocket where he'd deposited the card she'd received. "And you get one more message like this, I will throw you over my shoulder and carry you out of this place myself. Understood?"

Rebecca nodded.

Seth turned and walked away.

Chapter Eight

-

"What about the blonde?"

"I'm keeping an eye on her, just like you said. She refused the money. I don't know if she's greedy or if she's holding out for a diamond ring from Mr. Wolfe, but I—"

"*I* am Mr. Wolfe."

"Yes, sir. Of course, sir." Theodore Wolfe, Sr.'s American spy apologized, as he was expected to. He'd been a loyal enforcer of Wolfe International's interests for a long time. Long enough to know that he wasn't the only watchdog on Daddy's payroll, long enough to know that the secrets he was privy to would make him a liability if he ever fell out of favor with the boss. "As I was saying, I can confirm her efforts to extort money from Teddy. Though what specific evidence she's using against him, I can't say yet."

"Could there really be a grandchild?"

"She refused a pregnancy test. Even after some…insistent…urging. Makes me wonder if she really is carrying a child."

"Or if Teddy's the real father."

He drew the last puff on his thin cigar and dropped it to the pavement, grinding it out beneath his shoe. The light inside the apartment he was watching finally went out. The hour was late. *About time she went to bed.* He wouldn't have suspected that the pretty little bitch he'd been following was the type of woman to sleep around. She seemed so loyal—even to the point of foolishly endangering her own life. But then, he'd been wrong about a woman before—and that betrayal was still eating away inside him.

Good enough reason to concentrate on Theodore Wolfe's orders and not let the memories of creamy skin and soft pleas distract him from his work. He strolled toward the sleek, pricey rental car he'd borrowed for the night, forcing his attention back to the long-distance call on his cell phone. "I can get a sample of her blood and have it processed."

"Good thinking. If there is a child, I want it. If not…"

"I know what to do, Mr. Wolfe." He clicked the remote to unlock the car. "And my payment?"

"It will be there on time, just like it always is. Call me as soon as it's done."

He settled into the suede upholstery, removing his gun from inside his coat and placing it in the glove compartment before fastening his seat belt. "And if there is no baby?"

"Make the issue go away. I need Teddy to focus on business. I'm sure he can find another woman to warm his bed."

It wouldn't be the first time Teddy Wolfe had gotten himself into trouble.

It wouldn't be the last time *he'd* taken care of it.

"One more thing. It could be nothing, but—"

"What is it?"

"There's a new hire. A cocktail waitress. She's asking a lot of questions."

"About…?"

"Mostly about the old *Commodore*. But she's very… friendly."

"With Teddy?"

That old feeling of being used—of being mocked and betrayed behind his back filled his throat with bile and left him unable to speak for a moment. While she was definitely a pleasure to the eye, something about Rebecca Poochman didn't sit right. Maybe it was that idiotic name. Maybe it was the fact the woman didn't know her place in the order of things.

Or maybe it was those secret meetings she had with Seth Cartwright. The two were all friction on the surface, but mighty cozy when they got up close. It all added up to a lie on someone's part.

Probably the woman's.

"Let's just say she gets around more than a new hire should."

"Could be ambition. That can be an asset if it's channelled correctly."

He bit his tongue. Leave it to the Wolfes to excuse a woman's actions because of the size of her boobs or the length of her legs. Good thing he was made of sterner stuff. "It could work against you, too. Remember that."

"I'm forgetting nothing." The boss sounded perturbed that he'd challenged his wisdom. "Find out all you can about her. Keep me posted."

"Yes, sir."

"You're my eyes and ears and strong hand there. I pay you very well to do what needs to be done."

As if he needed the reminder. He started the car, savoring the strength of the engine purring beneath the hood. He liked being in control of all that power. Liked bending it to his will. There was something to be said for machines. They were so much more cooperative than people. He shifted the car into gear and pulled into the street.

"I haven't failed you yet."

"Wow. Only your second week on the job, and you've already got the hang of it." Melissa Teague glanced down the long countertop in the women's dressing room to Rebecca's reflection in the mirror. "You're changed and ready before I am."

Rebecca smoothed the draped folds of her dance-hall-girl costume over her hips, and hooked the black velvet choker in place. She was becoming a pro at dashing in at the last minute and making a quick change for work. Other than the feeling that Seth somehow always had her in his sights—either through a camera lens or across a crowded bar or gaming table—no one seemed to mind that she came in early to explore the ship or poke her nose around the personnel office or time the comings and goings of the Riverboat's major players.

She'd had no more secret meetings with Seth. No more kisses. No more pointed looks that got under her skin and made her forget she was here for her father. Other than his insistence that he drive her home when she got off work—and take her to get her car out of the shop tomorrow—he hadn't said a word. No teasing. No warnings. And certainly nothing *personal*.

Just watching.

She should be happy that he was finally leaving her alone to do her work. But it only made her suspicious about what he was up to. Was it legal? Safe? Could it get her closer to the truth about her father?

Though she hadn't yet found an opportunity to sneak back down to the engine room on her own, she'd memorized the layout of the entire casino from stem to stern. Austin had been a willing guide. Despite Seth's advice, she couldn't help but form an attachment to the older man. He was knowledgeable and charming— and he needed someone to care about him. Maybe it was guilt that led her to share breaks and trade winks with the older man, maybe it was a selfish need to recapture some of the camaraderie she'd once shared with her own father.

And it was already too late to pull back from her friendship with Melissa. Considering the cautious reserve the blond woman wore around her like a cloak, Rebecca had discovered they had a lot in common. A love for books. A shortage of close female friends. And both of them had lost their fathers—though Rebecca hadn't yet shared that particular piece of information about Reuben herself.

With her black-buttoned ankle boots already snapped into place, all Rebecca had left to complete her uniform for the night was to pin her black cap on top of the loose bun she'd gathered at the back of her head. "I've got the hang of everything except the feathers. I think the women here should unionize and put an end to these goofy headpieces. If the feathers aren't tickling my neck, then they're poking me in the eye.

"My favorite is when you bend over to pick up a drink and one of them dangles into the glass."

Rebecca laughed.

Melissa actually smiled, though it ended abruptly beneath a grimace of pain and she quickly moved away. No amount of makeup or ducking her head could completely mask the puffy abrasion on her left cheek. She massaged her temple as she retrieved a bottle of ibuprofen from her locker.

Rebecca had a bottle of water ready before Melissa dumped two tablets into her hand. She met her new best bud halfway to the minifridge and handed it over, shrugging off Melissa's self-conscious "Thanks." "That looks like it really hurts. Does it need a couple of stitches?"

Melissa swallowed the pills before answering. "The invisible adhesive is fine. I had an accident last night. Ran into a door."

Ran into a fist was more like it. Rebecca would love to take a tape measure and find the knuckles that matched the size of that bruise.

"Bad headache?"

"I've had it all day. I can't seem to shake it."

"Could be a concussion. You really should see a doctor. Although you shouldn't be driving. Let me take you." *Right now, without looking back, leave the River-boat short-handed and save yourself.*

"I need to work my shift."

It was past time to pretend there was nothing wrong here. "You know, Mel—there are people who can help you. Places you can go."

Melissa was beyond the point of pretending, too. "I know. But they just make things worse when I go back home."

"Then don't go back."

"I have a little boy and a mother. If I'm not here, then he'll go find them."

"Let me help you. We can pick up your son and mother, and we'll all go to the shelter together."

"Thanks, Rebecca. Really." She could already hear the *no* in Melissa's voice. "I appreciate you sticking your neck out for me. But he can hurt you, too."

"*He* who? Ace? Teddy? What did he say that upset you so much night before last?"

Melissa hesitated a moment. Her skin blanched beneath her makeup, making the colorful welt even more prominent. But, as before, she collected her composure and pasted on a serene expression. "Ace is a mistake from my past. We haven't been together for a long time."

"That doesn't mean he isn't the one hurting you."

"It's not his fault—"

"Don't you dare give me that. Report him. Or I will."

"I appreciate you taking me down to the Plaza yesterday, but that doesn't give you the right—oh-h-h…" Melissa stumbled on her way to the door. She clutched her head and stomach, swaying as she battled a wave of dizziness.

"Melissa!" Rebecca was right there to help her. She

grabbed an elbow and a hand, and tried to lead her to a bench, but Melissa straightened her legs beneath her and refused to sit.

"I'm okay."

"No, you're not." This was bad. Right now, she wished Seth *could* see her on one of his security cameras. Maybe having the tough guy around for backup would convince Melissa to seek help. He could give one of his terse commands, bundle her out the door and get her safely beyond Ace Longbow's reach. "Let me make a phone call. Please."

Melissa's hand tightened around Rebecca's, offering reassurance while taking strength. "Look. I'm not a complete idiot. I left Ace as soon as I realized what kind of man he was. But it's hard to walk away from these people once you know things, unless you have a lot of money or a lot of power. And I don't have either one."

Rebecca frowned. "So you just take it?"

Melissa winced, and Rebecca immediately regretted her bluntness. "I'm not strong like you." She squeezed Rebecca's hand and found the courage to smile. "I wish I was. I heard what happened to your car. Don't think that was a random accident. You shouldn't have stayed."

"If I find out who's doing this to you—"

"Then you'll be as mixed up in this as I am. They won't let you leave, either. Once you become a part of this place, there's a certain loyalty expected from you. That's what Teddy reminded me of."

"Information is power," Rebecca insisted. "Exposing the truth is the only way to protect yourself. And your family."

Melissa shook her head and smiled as though Rebecca was naive for clinging to that ideal. "Don't you read the papers or watch TV? Anyone who stands up to men like Teddy Wolfe and Ace winds up paying dearly. I won't risk my son's life. Or my mother's."

Rebecca's own stomach took a queasy turn. She knew all too well the consequences for standing up to a man like Teddy. She squeezed Reuben's ring inside the pocket of her mini-skirt, where she'd tucked it in along with her locker key. "There has to be something we can do."

"Tom will be waiting for us. We had better get to work."

Before Rebecca followed Melissa to the door, she had one more question to ask. "Was that you in Teddy's limo last week?"

Melissa paused, but since she didn't turn around, there was no way to gauge whether dizziness or denial colored her answer. "I don't know what you're talking about. We'd better get to work."

TOM SAWYER was on the phone behind the bar when they went into the Cotton Blossom to gather their trays and aprons. "Hey, ladies…" His greeting became an audible gasp when he saw Melissa's cheek. "You okay?"

Melissa nodded, but then clutched the edge of the bar and squeezed her eyes shut, convincing no one that she wasn't in serious pain.

Though Tom's curses sounded sincere, he turned his back to her, as if the sight of her swollen face bothered him. Did the beefy bartender have a soft heart or a guilty conscience? As the business on the phone demanded his attention, Rebecca wondered if *he* could be the beater. Melissa had refused to confirm either Ace or Teddy as her attacker. Maybe there were other candidates for her to consider. A sly look at Tom's knuckles revealed no scrapes or bruises, but even though summer was well underway, he could have worn gloves.

"Yes, sir. I'll send her right up." Tom completed his phone call and turned toward Melissa. "Mr. Wolfe is having a meeting in his office. He ordered some drinks and wants you to bring them up."

Melissa's tiny frame sagged with a weary sigh. She pushed to her feet, but quickly sank back onto the stool where she'd been sitting and massaged her temple. "Give me a minute."

This was crazy. Rebecca chimed in. "I'll go."

Tom dampened a towel with cool water from the ice bin and handed it to Melissa. "He specifically asked for Mel."

"Well, the big boss isn't getting what he wants this time. I'm going."

Sawyer hesitated, but not for long. "Okay." He dropped his voice to a whisper. "I'll keep my eye on her."

Melissa didn't hear the proprietary comment. Or else she was ignoring it. "Teddy drinks a vodka gimlet," she said, reciting the order by rote. "Mr. McDonough has a Scotch, neat. Mr. Kelleher will want a soda with a twist, and—"

"I know what they drink." Tom cut her off.

"I'm just trying to help."

"You help by sittin' tight and feelin' better."

Just a few efficient minutes later, Tom set the last drinks on Rebecca's tray.

"Be sure you knock first," Melissa advised. "But then you can go right in. They'll be talking business. Ignore it if you want. They'll probably ignore you."

Rebecca reached over to give Melissa's hand a reassuring squeeze. "I can handle a roomful of thirsty men."

She waited long enough to decide that Melissa showed no fear of Sawyer. Though she was showing little beyond being nauseous from the head injury. Plus, there were a half dozen customers already settling in around the tabletop slot machines. Nothing could happen to her with all these witnesses, right?

Rebecca carried the drinks up the grand staircase and turned left toward the suite of rooms that housed Teddy's office and private apartments. It was one of the few areas of the Riverboat she hadn't been able to explore yet. Hopefully, volunteering would serve two purposes—she could save Melissa from climbing the stairs and carrying a heavy tray, and she could case the office for any sort of useful evidence. Disks? Reports? Another briefcase with handcuffs and a large amount of money?

Like she'd be that lucky.

Nope, no luck at all.

Rebecca slowed her step as Dawn walked out of Teddy's office. Though it was well past the beginning of her shift, the young blond hostess wore low-slung jeans and a V-neck halter top cut low enough to reveal most of her ample bosom.

"What are you doing up here?" Dawn practically spat the accusation at her.

Now here was a friendship that *hadn't* panned out. "Serving drinks."

"Uh-huh." Interesting how two nonsense syllables could carry such meaning. "That better be all you're doing."

"Trust me, Dawn, I'm working." She inclined her head toward the diamond watch on Dawn's wrist. "You should hustle downstairs and get changed so you can do the same."

Should she even try to warn the young woman that she could wind up in the same predicament Melissa was in if she continued to be involved with these men?

"Just stay away from Teddy. He's mine."

"Guess not," Rebecca muttered.

"What?"

"Nothing. Have a good evening."

Dawn stopped beside Rebecca on her way down the stairs. "I'm watching you."

Even coming from a short, insecure blonde, that sounded like a threat. Rebecca paused long enough to watch Dawn bounce down the stairs. Could Dawn have trashed her Mustang in a jealous rage? That could explain the bright-red lipstick. Maybe the messages she'd received had nothing to do with her investigation and everything to do with a spiteful young woman.

But no way could that hulk following her through the shadows have been little Dawn. Even that rationalization couldn't prevent the sea of goose bumps that pricked along her arms as she rapped lightly on Teddy's office door.

She turned the knob and walked on in as Melissa had instructed, immediately taking note of every posh appointment. This wasn't an office so much as a luxury penthouse. All the Riverboat's chief personnel had gathered like the knights of some twisted Round Table, and Teddy Wolfe was king of his opulent domain.

A silent pulse of energy drew her gaze straight to the stocky man standing across the room behind Teddy's big walnut desk. Seth. She locked on to his shaded green eyes and read the silent message that went something like, *What the hell are you doing here? Get out. Now.*

We talked about this, she wanted to reply. *You can't scare me away from this story, nor can any other man in this room.* Then she swallowed hard and looked away from his probing gaze.

As she walked between the chairs and sofas and served their drinks, Rebecca quietly made note of the file cabinets and white-shuttered doors that could lead to walk-in closets or adjoining rooms. The bedroom area was separated from the office and seating area by nothing more than a Japanese bamboo screen.

Teddy was going on about the poker game and security expectations. How would the money be transported? He wanted an armed guard stationed at each exit. And how was the menu coming for the hors d'oeuvres, anyway?

Rebecca handed Shaw McDonough his Scotch. He seemed perturbed that he actually had to remove one of his hands from his jacket pocket to take the glass from her. She skirted around the pillar where Ace Longbow stood and approached the middle-aged man with the graying temples on the sofa. Daniel Kelleher.

He took his drink and voiced a question to Teddy. "Why aren't you televising the tournament? Three local stations offered to pay for coverage privileges. It'd be a sure profit whether we win or lose that card game."

"Always thinking about the bottom line, aren't you, Daniel?" Teddy drummed his fingers on top of his desk. "We're guaranteeing a certain degree of anonymity in order to bring in some truly big players. Without fifty grand up front, you can't even sit at the table."

"Can we afford to lose three million if the game goes south? We already have some accounts in the red as it is."

"This will be our big moneymaker," Teddy insisted.

As the debate continued, Rebecca moved on to the next man. Did he really need to be in here listening to all this talk about poker games with huge payouts? "Hey, Austin."

He winked his thanks.

She handed Seth his beer and got to Teddy last. She placed a coaster on his desk, read the encryption message on his computer monitor and spotted the briefcase with handcuffs beneath his desk before placing his vodka gimlet before him.

As she pulled away, he grabbed her wrist and yanked her back to his side. "You serve me first."

"I'm sorry." Rebecca's heart pounded in her chest, on guard against his touch, relieved by his words. She'd thought he'd caught her red-handed, snooping where she shouldn't. But no, this was once again about Teddy's ego. "You were busy with your instructions and I didn't want to interrupt."

"Who signs your paycheck?"

"You do."

"Then you serve me first."

Her wrist throbbed when he released her and her temper bloomed. He reached up and traced his finger along her bare collarbone and Rebecca flinched away, sickened more by the gentle touch on the heels of his violent outburst than by the violence itself.

"I asked for Melissa."

"Well, that makes me feel welcome," she snapped, moving beyond the reach of his hand.

Seth cleared his throat, warning her to choose her battles wisely.

"It's not that I don't enjoy your company." Teddy smiled as though his handsome face made up for anything he said or did. "It's just that when I ask for something, I expect it to be done. Isn't that true, gentlemen?"

An unsatisfactory rumble of consent answered him.

He pounded the desk with his fist. "Isn't that true!"

"Yes."

"Of course."

"Yes, Teddy."

"Right."

One of the five men didn't answer. But before she could pinpoint the rebel in the bunch, Teddy tucked his finger beneath the ruffles at her cleavage and pulled her forward. After that outburst, the European charm in his quiet tone was creepy. "Why didn't Melissa come in the first place?"

"She wasn't feeling well."

Ace suddenly advanced, startling her. "What's she complaining about now?"

Rebecca jumped in her boots, but found a warm, solid hand at the center of her back—calming her, supporting her.

"Back off, Ace." Seth's warning was friendly, low-pitched and convincing enough that even Rebecca trembled.

As the big Indian grumbled back to his shadow, she saw the bruises on his right knuckles. She couldn't help it. She had to ask, "How did you hurt your hand?"

Ace crossed his arms, hiding the injury, and leaned back against the pillar. He directed his words to Teddy and ignored her. "I thought we were having a meeting here."

Teddy rose from his chair and waved them all away. "We're done. You all know what to do. I expect everything to run perfectly this weekend. No mistakes, no distractions. Understood?"

"You won't be disappointed, Teddy," Shaw promised, herding the others with their drinks out the door ahead of him. "Let's go make some money, gentlemen."

Seth turned Rebecca to follow them out, but Teddy stopped them with a surprising invitation. "Rebecca— I'll be needing some of our most efficient and discreet staff to serve in the private rooms tomorrow night. The tips are fabulous. Interested?"

"Teddy—" Seth tried to intervene.

"Hey, he asked me, not you, tough guy." An opportunity to have free rein to explore the private suites upstairs? Rebecca counted to three so she wouldn't sound too eager to jump at the chance. "How fabulous?"

Teddy smiled. "Very."

She formed a smile of her own. "I'm in."

Seth's hand stayed on her waist as they walked back down the stairs. He leaned in to whisper, "You want to tell me what that appearance was all about?"

"Helping out a friend who's been hit in the head so hard that she can't stand up straight." Seth swore. Rebecca agreed. "What you said. Did you see Ace's hand?"

"He's been in a fight." Seth grabbed a handful of her bustle and pulled her up short at the bottom of the stairs. "I meant, what are you doing agreeing to serve at that party tomorrow? When Teddy says, 'efficient and discreet,' he's talking about pretty girls. Arm candy. He's not looking for waitresses. He's looking for escorts."

Chapter Nine

"Reuben Page."

Cooper Bellamy tossed the beat-up file folder into Seth's lap as soon as he climbed into the passenger seat of Coop's truck. He recognized the driver's license photo as the same man in the photograph on Rebecca Page's desk.

"Her father?" It was an old KCPD report. Seth opened the file and flipped through the meager contents, looking for anything that would help him understand Rebecca's purpose here. "How do I know that name?"

"He won a Pulitzer for writing a series of articles exposing organized crime in Chicago."

Cripes. Rebecca was trying to follow in her father's footsteps.

Seth lay the folder on the dashboard and looked outside at the Riverboat's parking lot. It was risky meeting his partner here, but with the five wealthy players arriving to spend the weekend playing poker with Teddy—and unbeknownst to them, help him launder over a million dollars worth of drug money into clean, untraceable, *legally* accounted cash—the demands on his time and security expertise were nonstop. Skipping out now to run a few miles or meet for a drink in a hole-in-the-wall bar would raise questions from the boss he didn't want to answer. The last thing he needed right now—when he had everything in place to record the game, the under-the-table transactions and the shifty accounting—was for Teddy to question his loyalty and take him off the front line where the action was certain to go down.

But Seth needed answers.

Because that stubborn, sexy, hold-on-to-him-tight Rebecca Page had maneuvered herself onto the front line of that poker game, too. And if her agenda got in the way of his, she could blow eight months worth of police work.

"So Rebecca's trying to take up where daddy left off. She's trying to make a name for herself."

"It's more than that. I think she—"

"Now what?" Seth grabbed the dash and leaned forward as a familiar car pulled into the parking lot. "Sarah?"

Had Austin gotten himself into some other kind of trouble? Though Seth had long ago written off his father as a man worth helping through the day-to-day crises he seemed to get himself into, his sister was a gentle soul who had a hard time saying no. A hard time walking away from anyone she cared about. Seth reached for the door handle. "I'd better go see what the trouble is this time."

Coop's low wolf whistle stopped Seth even before he saw Sarah climb out of her car. What the...? What was she wearing? What happened to her usual tomboy attire?

"Wow." Coop's obvious approval made Sarah's intention clear. "The schoolmarm dolls up real sweet. I don't think I've ever seen her in a dress."

Seth tore his gaze away from the upswept hair and shoulder-baring sundress and punched Coop's shoulder. "If you weren't my partner, my best friend… if my life wasn't still in your hands for the next few days, I'd lay you flat out."

Coop raised his hands in surrender. "Hey, I'm just being an observant detective. So what if your twin sister puts on a little lipstick? I still think of her as the left-fielder who ran down that final out in our coed softball game against the fire department last summer. Hitting on your sister is a no-no. I get that."

"That's non-negotiable, Coop."

"Understood." Relegated to big-brother status, Coop asked the same question Seth had been thinking. "So what's she doing here at the Riverboat, dressed for action?"

Seth reached for the door handle. "I intend to find out."

"Hold on, tiger." Coop picked up the file and flipped to the last page, forcing Seth to stop worrying about his sister and start concentrating on his work. "I've been up twenty-four hours puttin' this report together. You missed the best part. Reuben Page moved to Kansas City and started writing for the *Journal* about ten years ago. Three years ago he was found murdered right here on the decks of the old *Commodore*. The shooter was never found, a motive never proven." He pointed to a blond woman's photo. "Danielle Ballard, died the same night. Same dock. The MOs were different—she was knifed, he took a bullet to the head—but my gut says the two murders are connected. The time and location are too close together to be a coincidence."

Coop's reasoning made sense. "So Rebecca's out for revenge?"

"Revenge on whom? Both murders were transferred to the cold-case section earlier this year. The killer was never found."

Seth swore up one side and down the other. He'd suspected all along she wasn't writing any damn history article. But now he had proof.

She was trying to solve her father's murder.

REBECCA SWATTED the man's hand from her rear. Gilbert Cho seemed inexplicably amused each time she did that. But grabbing and swatting meant he kept asking her back for drink refills. And Rebecca had already heard enough enlightening chatter upstairs in Teddy Wolfe's private rooms that she'd put up with whatever was necessary to spend time there.

"C'mon, Teddy, you know I'm good for it." Austin Cartwright mopped the perspiration from his forehead with his white handkerchief. "Haven't I always come through for you?"

Teddy, by contrast, still looked fresh and pressed as he considered his cards on the opposite side of the table. "You're already down by two-hundred grand. What makes you think I'm going to cover this bet for another sixty?"

"I'm due for a winner. Everybody at this table knows it."

"Maybe it's time for a break," Rebecca suggested. "It's been a long night."

She squeezed his shoulder before clearing away his empty glass, hoping a friendly show of support would give him the courage to walk away from the table before his situation got any worse. But his skin was feverish to the touch beneath his rumpled white shirt, his muscles tense with the desperation of his obsession.

Austin couldn't hear her. His eyes were fixed on Teddy, his enabler. Or in Austin's mind, his salvation.

Teddy glanced up over Austin's head to Rebecca. "We'll break after this hand."

Was that a reprimand? Or did that smug smile that curled his lips mean he thought he was doing her a favor by granting her suggestion?

Whatever the eye contact meant, Dawn didn't like it. The petite blonde, who'd draped herself over a nearby couch to read a magazine while five hours of poker went by, quickly swung to her feet and lay a freshly manicured hand on Teddy's shoulder. She flashed a sapphire ring to go with the diamond watch now. She even twisted around to perch on Teddy's thigh when Melissa reached in to freshen his drink, and Rebecca had to turn away to forestall a snicker at the young woman's possessive insecurity.

"I want to play until I've won all your money," Gilbert teased. "Or I have lost all of mine." There was a general consensus of yeses and joking around the table.

The only player who wasn't laughing was Austin.

For him, this wasn't a game. It seemed more like a matter of life or death. Thank God Seth wasn't here to see his father reduced to this. But then, that was probably why Seth had opted to oversee the game's security from the command center in his office and leave uniformed men to actually guard the suite doors. Maybe there'd been scenes like this before. Rebecca's heart squeezed in her chest for both father and son. They'd both lost so much—time together, trust— maybe even love—to Austin's addiction. No wonder Seth had written his father off. It was probably far less heartbreaking to put the pain and loss out of his life than it was to deal with it day in and day out.

"Don't worry, Gilbert. I will give you a chance to lose as much as you like to me." Teddy stroked Dawn's back while his gaze reverted to Austin. "Let's call it a night and resume the game tomorrow after dinner. Is that a suitable compromise?"

Another player, a retired Southern gentleman, took Melissa Teague by the elbow, and pulled her back to his side. He picked up a hundred-dollar chip and set it on her tray. "You'd better cancel that last drink, honey. But you done real good tonight." He held up a second chip between his fingers. "You gonna be here to wait on me tomorrow?"

Melissa grinned and batted at the brim of his Stetson. "I sure will, Freddie."

"If Mel's coming, I'll be back."

She snatched the chip from his fingers and held her smile until she passed by the scowling behemoth who had once been her husband. One contemptible glare from Ace and Melissa's smile vanished. Her posture

sagged with fatigue by the time she reached the re-
freshment cart by the door to empty her tray. Rebecca
hurried over to help her—as much for moral support
as to ease the physical stress of working such a long
shift while injured and fighting her upset stomach.

There was a general agreement from among the
others at the table. The hour was late, funds needed to
be counted, strategies reassessed.

Austin pounded the table with his fist. "I want to
play this hand!"

The room instantly fell silent. Shaw pushed to his feet
from behind Teddy's desk. Daniel Kelleher looked up
from the laptop where he'd been working. Ace took a
step forward, but Teddy raised a hand and warned him
back. "You know what I want. Win or lose, you'd owe
me."

Austin deliberated the unspoken offer, and Rebecca
wondered what the asking price was. Did his debt
involve loan sharks and broken legs? Or the comple-
tion of some unpleasant task on Teddy's behalf? Austin
stared at his cards, rubbing his hands over his jaw the
same way she'd seen Seth do so many times before.

"Is your hand that good?" Teddy prompted.

Placing the five cards face-down on the table in
front of him and covering them with his hand, Austin
finally nodded. "They're that good."

Gilbert, Freddie and the others immediately tossed
in their cards, some scoffing, others commenting on
the ups and downs of the game.

Teddy alone held on to his hand. "Suffice to say,
bluffing isn't a strength of yours, is it?" The others
laughed. Rebecca wanted to cry out at the pathetic

figure they were making of Austin. "I'll cover your wager per our agreement. And I'll call."

One by one, he laid five spades on the table—3-4-5-6-7.

The room collectively held its breath. Austin visibly shook as he crushed the cards beneath his hand.

"Show me your cards, Austin."

With a halting curse that sounded more like a plea for his life, Austin turned over his cards. Four jacks.

Teddy expelled a breath as if all the tension in the room bored him.

He scooted Dawn off his lap and stood. "Let's call it a night."

Rebecca was no poker expert, but the reactions of everyone in the room made it clear—Teddy had won.

Austin stared sightlessly at the center of the table, defeated in more ways than one. Rebecca wanted to go to him, but the others were getting up, scattering. Going about their business as though Austin's humiliation was of no concern to them.

"Goodnight, everyone." Teddy leaned over the table. "I'll expect payment tonight, old friend."

Austin barely nodded.

At least he was alive. He was $260,000 in debt to Teddy Wolfe, but he was alive. That was a good thing, right? Why wasn't he getting up and moving around like everyone else?

"Keep working." Melissa's soft whisper and gentle touch on her arm broke Rebecca's sympathetic spell. "You can't help him now."

"Gentlemen, check your chips with Daniel." While Rebecca and Melissa cleared and cleaned, Teddy gave directions to his guests as he ushered them out. "He'll log in the balance and give you a receipt for tomorrow. If you wish to add to your total at that time, you may. Our security chief will provide each of you with a private escort back to your hotel. If you'd like to play at the tables downstairs for a while yet, let him know. I want each of you to get home safely. Until tomorrow, enjoy your stay in Kansas City."

"You're not sending me home, are you, Teddy?" Dawn asked.

He stopped up her mouth with a quick kiss, then turned her toward the door. "Go change into something more…comfortable. Come back and wait for me in the bedroom."

"Right." Beaming with anticipation if not completely restored confidence, Dawn stretched up on tiptoe to kiss him. "I'll be there."

Amidst the bustle of activity around Kelleher and his laptop, and players hanging back to chat with Teddy or their favorite cocktail waitresses, Shaw McDonough nodded to Ace. Without a word, Ace crossed to Austin's chair, stood over him until the older man finally roused himself to stand and retrieve his jacket, and escorted him from the room.

Fifteen minutes later, the guests were gone and Daniel Kelleher was closing his laptop. "We're up a million six. Even with expenses, that puts us in the profit margin. Once you repay the stake that Wolfe International fronted you, then we're guaranteed a minimum of—"

"Daniel." Shaw McDonough shushed the financial report with one crisp word and a pointed glance in

Rebecca's direction. "We'll discuss business affairs later."

She'd already sent Melissa down to the bar with the first load of dirty glasses. Her friend was dragging, and Rebecca hoped to finish the rest of their duties before Mel had to come back. Though her ears were as attuned to the conversation as Shaw expected, Rebecca concentrated on folding the used towels and other linens as though it was the most fascinating task imaginable.

Kelleher dropped his voice to an equally urgent whisper. "We can't put this off. London is expecting a report from me in the morning. And you know damn well the police and the IRS are keeping an eye on a tournament as big as this one. All our figures have to look perfect."

Shaw nodded. "You're right to be concerned, of course." He reached for the laptop. "Why don't you let me have a look at things tonight? I'll handle London in the morning."

Daniel held fast. "These are only rough figures."

"Understood." A polite tug-of-war was on. "They're only looking for profit or no profit at this point. Not details."

"Fine." He let Shaw have the laptop, but pulled a disk from his pocket to show he wasn't truly giving in. "I have my own copy. I'll work on these tonight. I don't know how they run a business in London. But here, details are everything. I'll file the report in the morning."

"Gentlemen." Teddy rested a hand on either man's shoulder and acted as friendly referee. "Don't you trust Shaw?" he asked of Daniel. The American straightened without answering. Teddy smiled. "I don't trust Shaw, either."

The thick-necked Brit shot an accusatory gaze at Teddy. "I've been with your father's company for years."

"Yes, well I've been a Wolfe all my life." His expression changed from charming to impatient to downright irritated before his smile reappeared. "I'll take both of these. And then I'll speak to Father in the morning. He'll be pleased to know that *I'm* in charge here."

Period. Done. End of conversation.

Despite the clear displeasure of both men, Shaw and Daniel left the room. Teddy opened the laptop on his desk and lit one of his long brown cigarettes before inserting the disk.

If only Teddy had left with them. Rebecca would have risked a look at those laptop files. But alone with Teddy wasn't the best place for her to be, so she hastily stuffed the last of her linens into the cart and leaned over to unlock the brakes.

By the time she straightened back up, Teddy had walked up behind her. "You did a fine job tonight, Rebecca."

She gripped the cart's handle to mask being startled. "Yes, well, I'd best get this downstairs so I can finish the job."

He reached around, stopping her with a hand on her wrist.

"Don't be in such a hurry to leave me." The pungent aroma of smoke tried to spark a memory in her. Was it the same fragrance she'd smelled in the parking lot the night she'd been followed? This scent seemed stronger. But then, she'd been outdoors. Its strength could have dissipated or been altered by the breeze off the river. Teddy pressed himself against her back, trapping her against the cart. "You make me think that you don't like me."

Rebecca clenched her teeth to control her tongue. Teddy liked to flirt. He liked to talk when he had a captive audience. "You're a handsome man."

If looks were all that counted, it wasn't a lie.

"And you're a beautiful woman." He rubbed himself suggestively against her, and Rebecca did flinch. "Shh."

He thought he made her nervous. But he would never grasp the distinction between fear and revulsion, and feminine anticipation. "Teddy, I have work to do."

"We've had this discussion before." He blew a puff of smoke past her ear before nibbling on the lobe. "You serve my needs first."

He folded one hand over her arm and massaged it much the same way Seth had. But where she'd found comfort and excitement in Seth's touch, Teddy's seduction was all about power and control. Rebecca wildly searched the room for any glimpse of a camera. For once in her life, she wanted that short, combative alpha-male security chief to barge in and take over the situation.

But Seth wasn't here. It wasn't his job to protect her. She'd come into this investigation alone. And, by God, if it meant tapping into the reserves of strength and will she'd inherited from her father, then she'd take care of this predicament. Alone.

She lifted her hand to push his mouth from her ear. "This isn't a good time for me."

"Don't be coy." He moved his hand over her shoulder to her collarbone, and slid a poker chip down the front of her dress. "Consider that a down payment. I know how to treat a lady very well. What is it you want? Jewelry? A sports car?"

Would answers about her father's murder be an option?

Hell. Why not?

Ignoring the dirty way he made her feel, Rebecca asked. "How about information?"

He laughed against her neck. "I'm six-four. Thirty years old. Embarrassingly wealthy—"

Rebecca forced some space between them and turned. "I meant about your company. I've heard some interesting talk around the casino. I heard you had to bribe someone on the city's Economic Development Committee to get permission to build and invest in Kansas City."

Bingo. He smiled down at her, seemingly impressed with her daring and savvy. "We greased a palm here and there. It's standard practice."

Not in her town. Not on her father's watch.

"What about men who can't be bribed?"

He touched her top hook at her neckline and unfastened it. "Money is a universal language. Everybody wants more than they have." *Not everybody.* He moved on to the next hook. "If money isn't convincing enough, there's more than one way to deal with those who stand in your way. Some philosophers call it the balance of power. But a smart businessman always keeps the power in his favor."

Curling into herself to avoid skin-to-skin contact, Rebecca followed up with another question. "Did anyone else stand in your way? Of all this amazing success?" she added to keep his ego guiding his tongue.

She kept her lips pressed tight as he brushed his mouth against hers. "Not everyone likes the presence of big gambling. Not even everyone in the company wanted us to come to the States." He pressed his mouth more firmly against hers. "But I'm glad we did."

Rebecca put a finger to his lips to push some distance between them. "What about this 'balance of power?' What happened to those people who spoke out against you?"

He shook his head and pulled her into his body. "Don't be against me and you won't have to find out."

"You get tough with them, hmm? I like a man who knows how to be strong."

"Why are we talking business? I pay people good money to take care of enemies and inconveniences for me." So which was her father? An enemy? An inconvenience? While Rebecca bit her tongue and seethed, he nuzzled her neck. "I'm bored with Dawn. Eager as she is to please me, I want something fresh and exciting. I know a mature, modern woman like you would know how to have a no-strings affair. What are you doing tonight?"

Rebecca wedged her fists between them. "I thought you invited Dawn to spend the night."

"Not the whole night."

Rebecca pushed. Her stomach couldn't take any more of this. "I don't want to stay."

"I think you do."

A knock at the door saved Teddy from a knee to the groin.

"Damn intrusion. Go away!" Teddy shouted.

"It's Austin."

Teddy's whole demeanor changed for an instant. His grip hurt. His eyes flashed.

"I brought what you asked," Austin spoke through the door.

Teddy suddenly relaxed. He released Rebecca and took another draw of his thin cigar before reaching around her to put it out in a glass. He arched an eyebrow. "You missed your chance."

Dodged a bullet was more like it.

Rebecca touched Reuben's ring in her pocket and sent up a silent prayer of thanks that Teddy had left her to answer the door. She quickly refastened her top and gathered her things, giving one last longing look at the laptop before rolling the cart toward the door. At least she knew for certain that Wolfe International had dealt with people who'd worked against their coming to K.C. Whether or not that meant Teddy had killed her father—or paid someone to have him killed—couldn't be proven yet. But at least she was now certain he was capable of such a crime.

Now all she wanted was to get home to shower the crawly aftereffects of Teddy's touch from her body, put on something comfy and curl up with her father's notebook to update her suspicions.

But the conversation at the open door stopped her short.

"Of course, I remember Sarah."

Oh. My. God.

Teddy stood in the doorway, greeting Sarah Cartwright with his usual kiss-the-hand routine. "I'm glad
you decided to take me up on my offer."

She looked so pretty. So sweet. So guileless in a way
that Seth had forgotten long ago. And dammit, judging
by the blush on her cheeks, she was eating up all of
Teddy's attention.

Sarah pulled her hand away, thinking a joke
would put off his intentions. "Down, boy. We're just
talking about a tour, right? Dad has talked a lot about
the Riverboat. I'd love to see behind the scenes. I
teach my fourth-graders Missouri history. I think
the mix of old and modern in this place would fascinate them."

"I'll do my best to fascinate." Teddy grinned,
drawing her into his deceptive web. "Why don't you
step inside and wait a few minutes? I need to clear
some business off my desk, and then I'll show you all
the best—secret—places in the casino."

And Austin, damn him, stood a couple of feet
behind his daughter, making no effort to warn her off,
making no effort to set guidelines with Teddy. He'd
brought Sarah up here like a sacrifice to the gods.

Payback.

$260,000 in cash. Or a night with his daughter?

Rebecca was going to be sick. Someone had to
speak up.

"Sorry. Excuse me." She pulled the door open wide
and steered the cart into the hall, forcing Teddy to let
go so Sarah could back out of the way. "Hey, Sarah.
Good to see you again. Rebecca, remember?"

"Of course, I remember. They're not working you too hard here, are they?"

Rebecca rolled her eyes. "Slave-drivers. Every last one of them. But I'm about to get off." Under any other circumstance, this would have been a friendly, get-acquainted girl-to-girl chat. But Rebecca just wanted Sarah to leave with her. "Hey, you want to take me up on that drink? I'm doing some historical research myself. I'd love to compare notes."

"I'd like that." Sarah nodded. Rebecca hoped. "But maybe another time?"

"No time like the present."

Teddy gave Rebecca a little push out the door. "You have work to finish. You two ladies can make plans for tomorrow. I've been looking forward to getting to know Sarah better myself."

Sarah seemed startled when Teddy took her by the elbow and pulled her through the doorway. "Oh, um— tomorrow works for me. Give me a call. Seth or Dad will have my number."

"Excellent." Teddy was pushing the door shut.

Rebecca wedged her boot over the threshold. "Sarah?"

"Goodnight." Teddy looked beyond Rebecca. "Austin?"

In the ultimate betrayal, Austin pulled the cart back, tugging Rebecca off balance long enough for the door to close. She knocked. "Sarah?"

Their indistinct voices retreated farther into Teddy's suite. Rebecca rattled the doorknob, but it was locked. Maybe she was overreacting to the danger here. Maybe not.

She whirled around and shoved the cart out of her way. It hit the far wall, rattling glasses and spilling leftover drinks. "What kind of father are you?"

Austin seemed to have no energy even to argue with her. "Teddy asked if I could set him up for a date with Sarah. She's a pretty girl when she puts her mind to it. She could do worse."

"Not much."

"This is their first date. They'll just talk. Flirt a little." He dabbed at his forehead with his handkerchief. "He's not going to try anything he shouldn't."

Rebecca was outraged on Sarah's behalf. "Teddy's a player. He does things he *shouldn't* all the time."

"Sarah's a bright girl. She won't let it go too far."

"She's your daughter. He just put the moves on me in there less than five minutes ago. He terrorizes Melissa. And no telling what lies he's feeding Dawn. Protect her from that creep."

"I can't. I owe him too much."

Rebecca couldn't hide her disgust. "You put a price on your daughter's head?"

"According to Teddy, everybody's head has a price." Finally shrugging off his own self-loathing or whatever had him in that near-catatonic state, Austin stuffed his handkerchief back into his pocket and lifted his gaze to Rebecca's. "Sarah will come through. She'll take care of herself. She's strong like her mother and brother. If Teddy gets out of line, she'll tell him off."

"My father would be outraged. He would never let me be used or hurt like that." She was ashamed that she'd ever felt sorry for Austin. "You aren't any better a man than Teddy is."

He nodded. "I gave up any claim of being a good man a long time ago."

"Austin…!" Rebecca shook her fists in frustration.

If he was just going to wander back down to the casino, she would turn elsewhere for help. Leaving her cart and any pretense of role-playing behind, she hurried down the hall to the security offices.

Seth would want to know about this. Seth would help.

But his door was closed, the entire suite of offices nearly deserted. And she had no idea of a cell phone number or any other way to reach him.

"Rebecca?" LaTonya Marshall walked out of one of the rooms and met her at the reception desk. "May I help you with something?"

"Have you seen Seth? Is he around?" Rebecca forced herself to take a deep breath and gather her composure. That breathless impatience made her sound a little more reliant on Seth than she'd like anyone to know—than she'd like to admit to herself. "I have something I'd like to discuss with him."

LaTonya smiled sympathetically. "He's a busy man tonight. Right now he's escorting our special guests back to their hotels. It may be twenty or thirty minutes before he gets back." After twenty or thirty minutes, Sarah would either be beyond his help or home free. "I can call him if it's an emergency."

Um. Your sister's on a blind date set up by your father to get him out of hock with Teddy? Not the sort of message she wanted to leave on the phone. Or have his office assistant hear.

"No, that's okay. Could you just tell him I was looking for him? I'll catch up with him later."

"Of course I will."

Rebecca left the security suite, pulling out the chain with her father's ring and looping it around her neck for the sense of calm it afforded her. She sorted through her options. Did she make a pest of herself at Teddy's door? Did she trust—as Austin apparently did—that Sarah could handle herself with Teddy? Was it even her business to worry about Seth's sister being hurt—emotionally, possibly physically? Or should she just stick to deciphering her father's clues, find a way back into the engine room, grab whatever was in that compartment and hide someplace as far away as possible from the Riverboat to write her story?

Just thinking about the possibility of leaving before justice was done made Reuben's ring burn against her skin. She hadn't abandoned Melissa. She wouldn't abandon Sarah. She couldn't give up on the story here before she'd uncovered every truth.

"Teddy?" A sharp pounding on the door at the opposite end of the hall almost made Rebecca smile. Almost. "Teddy!"

She wouldn't have to worry about Sarah Cartwright at all as long as Dawn kept banging on the locked door.

"I know you have another woman in there. It's that slut, Rebecca, isn't it? Oh."

Rebecca crossed her arms and stood there, waiting for the stunned expression on Dawn's face to reach her brain. She wasn't insulted. If anything, she felt as sorry for Dawn as she'd once felt for Austin. It had to hurt to care so much about a man who had no qualms about betraying her with other women. Still, Dawn wrapped her silk robe tighter around her waist and tried to pretend she was still in control of some part of her life. "Well, you've made yourself right at home here, haven't you?"

"Walk away from him, Dawn. Teddy's just using you. You're a sweet girl. You deserve better."

She shook her loose golden hair off her face. "You don't know anything. You're just trying to get me out of your way. Do you really think I'm that stupid?"

"That naive, perhaps." Rebecca retrieved her cart, weary of fighting an argument she couldn't win. "I swear to you, I'm not interested in Teddy."

"Yeah? Well, I am." She knocked on the door while Rebecca headed toward the service elevator. "Teddy!"

A door opened farther down the hall, but Dawn was too busy defending her status to notice Shaw McDonough coming down the hall behind her. "I can give him something no other woman can. A real family. Real love."

"Teddy wouldn't know real love if it hit him in the face." Rebecca met Shaw's cold-eyed gaze and shivered herself. "Walk away, Dawn. Please."

"You're just jealous. Does he give you presents? Does he make love to you?"

"I'll handle this, Miss Poochman." Shaw wrapped his hand around Dawn's arm. She jumped, screeched at the unexpected touch. Twisted against his grip to no avail. "Listen to me." He shook her, his staunch British voice never wavering. "Mr. Wolfe is busy right now."

"He wants to see me," she insisted.

"You're making a spectacle of yourself." Something in his face—not a warning so much as pity—a desire to help—finally stilled her protests. "Come with me."

"We're going to his rooms the back way?"

There was another entrance?

Rebecca continued in the opposite direction as Shaw and Dawn walked side-by-side down the hall.

"We'll turn you into a lady again. Give you a few moments to calm yourself, freshen your lipstick and hair."

"And then we'll see Teddy?"

"If that's what you want." Shaw McDonough sounded so unexpectedly solicitous that Rebecca paused to look over her shoulder. That he happened to be looking over his shoulder at the same moment made Rebecca a little uneasy. But he'd actually managed to summon a smile for her. "Good night, Miss Poochman."

"Good night."

He opened the door he'd come out of and disappeared inside with Dawn.

If the whole past hour of her life hadn't been so incredibly weird and stressful, Rebecca would have breathed a sigh of relief. A second entrance to Teddy's private suite meant the rooms were connected. Sarah wasn't completely alone with Teddy. And Dawn had Shaw to look after her. Their presence should surely be enough to keep Teddy behaving like a gentleman. If not, they provided Sarah with an easy excuse to leave.

Rebecca's conscience gave her a momentary break. She was alone up here in the second-floor hallway. So long as the other two women were not, they should be safe enough.

Besides, Seth would be back soon enough to make sure that everything was as okay as Rebecca hoped.

Downstairs, once she'd delivered her cart, Rebecca quickly changed into her jeans and tennis shoes. She checked her father's notebook, her keys and her pepper spray before looping her bag over her shoulder and neck and heading out through the casino. Her Mustang still needed a few coats of paint, but the graffiti had been sanded away, and the damaged parts replaced. That part of her father was with her again. She would feel safe inside it for the few miles she had to drive to get home.

Then she could wash Teddy and the rest of tonight's mess off her, and curl up in the secure—if empty— confines of her apartment.

At two in the morning, things were definitely winding down at the Riverboat. With state and city ordinances closing them at one, the parking lot had already cleared except for the staff and patrons too drunk to be allowed to drive. Once Rebecca hit the peak of the gangplank, she spotted her car. Sure, it was almost a city block away on the far side of the lot, but it was a straight shot with plenty of wide open space between it and her—with no tight places for shadows to hide.

With a nod to the valets closing up shop for the night, Rebecca started to make her way across the parking lot.

"What are you turnin' to him for?"

The low-pitched threat from down near the water didn't startle her half as much as the thud and soft moan that followed.

Rebecca stuttered to a halt, turning her head to pinpoint the sound. She thought she heard something scraping across the gravel on the service walkway that ran beneath the gangplank and followed the bend in the river.

She looked back at the valets, trading stories about their night as they locked up their booth and headed back to the front doors. If they weren't concerned, maybe she had no reason to be, either. The night had just been too long, and her nerves were too frayed to control her imagination.

Clutching her pepper spray in one hand and her keys in the other, she resumed the walk to her car.

"I swear to God, Ace…" The muffled protest fought for volume. "Nothing happened between us."

"You lie."

A scream.

Ace?

"Melissa." She mouthed the name, turned toward the river.

"I didn't say a word." The soft voice was somewhere below her, pleading now. "He doesn't know."

"Liar."

"I didn't betray—"

Scream. Thud. Silence.

A mix of blind panic and rage hit Rebecca like a lightning bolt. She tucked her spray into her jeans, dug into her bag for her phone and spun toward the edge of the gangplank. "Melissa!"

The scuffle below her continued without further protest.

Like hell.

"Melissa!"

Rebecca ran to the railing. Her thumb hit a nine. A one. The arch of the gangplank cast shadows on the pathway beneath it, making it difficult to find the source of the violent, one-sided confrontation she could hear below her. Water lapped against the giant white rocks lining the bank. Even the bright lights of the casino couldn't penetrate the murky river or shadows cast by a webwork of steel support cables and anchoring pylons.

If Melissa was down there…

Has to be done. "Hey! Hey!"

She punched the second one, gave one last glance at the Riverboat's empty front doors and scrambled down the concrete stairs leading to the walkway.

"You've reached 9-1-1 assistance. How may I direct your call?"

Rebecca pulled the phone from her ear to catch herself as her foot slipped on the silt dusting the bottom steps. "Melissa? Answer me."

A flash of movement caught her eye. A jacket maybe. Or the hem of a skirt swinging out as the figure rounded the curve in the embankment and disappeared from sight.

"Hello?"

With rocks on one side and a metal fence on the other, there was little place to go except over the edge into the water. Thrusting the phone back to her ear, Rebecca hurried along the path. "I need the police. I'm at the Riverboat Casino."

She followed the crunching sound of running footsteps around the corner, past the sign marking the bridgeway over the river to the power unit entrance.

"What is the nature of your emergency?" the pleasant, professional voice droned in her ear.

"Somebody's beating the crap out of…" A swath of golden hair finally caught the light. Rebecca's stomach churned and dropped to her feet. "I need an ambulance. My name's Rebecca Page and I need an ambulance now."

She quickly scanned the shadows and, seeing no signs of movement, knelt beside the prone figure lying still against the fence. "Oh, my God."

Tears stung her eyes, but there was no time to cry. Rebecca pressed her fingers to the cool skin at Melissa Teague's neck. She gasped in a mixture of mourning and relief. Shock, maybe. But she could detect a pulse.

"Melissa?" She gently rolled her friend over. One eye was swollen shut, her mouth was bleeding and her injured wrist was now clearly broken. But Rebecca called to her, anyway. "Melissa? You hang on. I'm calling an ambulance."

"You just won't stay away from things that don't concern you, will you, bitch?"

The giant shadow materialized on the bridgeway behind her. Before Rebecca could scream, before she could stand, Ace Longbow grabbed her ponytail and yanked her to her feet. He threw her against the rocks, knocking the wind from her chest and the phone from her hand.

Feeling every rock like a fist to her back and legs, Rebecca sank to her hands and knees. Bits of gravel cut into her palms.

"Melissa's *my* business. She's *my* wife."

The sarcastic urge to point out the technicality of the

Longbows' divorce told Rebecca her strength was coming back. She sucked in a painful rasp of breath, reached into her pocket.

A zillion pinpricks of pain radiated across her scalp as Ace pulled her up by the hair. "You give her ideas like she can—"

Rebecca swung on around, spray in hand, and fired the caustic mist into Ace's eyes.

He cursed and released her. Rebecca found her balance and her voice as Ace covered his face and staggered into the fence. "I fight back, you bastard."

While Ace stumbled down the path, cursing her with every crude term imaginable, Rebecca frantically searched for something with a longer reach to defend herself. There. Not much. But something. She picked up a warped two-by-four that had been left to rot beside the path and positioned herself between Melissa and Ace.

Even in the dimness of the shadows, she could see the red burns that marked his face as he stalked toward her again. "Stay away," she warned.

"Make me."

Rebecca swung.

Ace caught the makeshift bat and jerked it from her grip, raking slivers across her fingers and nearly pulling her off her feet. Rebecca scooted back against the fence. "You're nothin' but mouth. And I'm gonna shut it up."

"Longbow." Ace froze at the distinctive sound of a bullet sliding into the chamber of a semiautomatic pistol. Or maybe it was the cold, deadly, unmistakable threat in Seth Cartwright's voice that made the big

Indian drop the wood and raise his hands in surrender. "I've been waiting for this moment a long time. Get away from her. Turn around nice and slow. And if I see your hand going anywhere near your gun, I'm gonna blow it off."

Chapter Ten

Ace Longbow was such a big bastard that Seth couldn't even see Rebecca from this angle. But the idiot had muscles for brains, and when he came around swinging, Seth easily ducked the attack.

He was almost glad Ace hadn't gone for his gun because there was something uniquely satisfying about a punch to the gut, another to the groin and a neat right hook to the giant's face. Ace's nose popped and he dropped to the ground, cradling his broken nose and bruised jewels with equal pain and despair.

Seth's pulse was still drumming in his ears the way it had when he first saw Ace raising that two-by-four to strike Rebecca. The tension in him had built from the moment LaTonya had informed him that Rebecca needed him. She'd come looking for him?

Either the woman was desperate for help, she'd uncovered something she shouldn't or she was responding to the same connection that drew him to her time and again. Any one of those was reason enough for Seth to hurry his search through the casino. She hadn't turned up in the bar or the women's dressing room, but

the valets in the lobby had seen her walking to her car.
Seth had run outside to find her, feeling the tension
coiling tighter and tighter inside him with every step.
But there was no leggy brunette in the parking lot. No
nosy reporter lurking in the shadows. Worry had
crawled up his gut as he feared the worst. Who had she
ticked off this time? What crazy predicament had she
gotten herself into?

And then he'd heard the sounds below him. Louder
than the beat of the river against the bank.

I fight back.

Bless that big mouth of hers.

Relief turned to fear so quickly that Seth was almost
light-headed by the time he hit the walkway. But when
he spotted Melissa on the ground, heard Rebecca's
brave words and saw Ace dare to threaten his...what?
His ally in all this mess? His equal? His *woman?*

The proprietary notion felt as foreign as it felt
right. Of all the women on the planet Seth could feel
something for, Rebecca Page should be at the bottom
of the list. Somehow, though, she'd pushed her way
to the top.

But before he could get his feelings sorted out,
before he could get away from all the lies of this damn
assignment and think straight, he had to stop Ace
Longbow from hurting her.

Yeah, with all that confusion roiling inside him, it
felt mighty good to finally give Ace Longbow a taste
of his own bullying terror.

Seth rolled him over and handcuffed him. He really
needed a second pair to hold the brute. But he'd settle
for relieving Ace of his gun and tucking it in the back

of his belt—and threatening more damage if he tried to give anyone anymore trouble.

He holstered his own weapon and called Riverboat security on his walkie-talkie. With the cavalry on its way to provide backup, Seth squatted beside Rebecca who was trying to stop the bleeding on Melissa's face by pressing her wadded-up tank-top over the reopened gash on her cheek.

"Bec?"

She knelt there in her bra, with that clunky ring caught inside one silky white cup, more concerned about her injured friend than the chill off the water or any immodest expanse of exposed skin. She sniffed back a sob, though Seth saw no tears. "I think she's in shock. It's been forever since I had first aid, though."

Melissa might not be the only one going into shock. Seth quickly shed his suit jacket, intending to cover Rebecca's shoulders, but she took the coat and tucked it around Melissa.

Stubborn woman.

Something inside Seth splintered open. He almost smiled at her tender-hearted practicality.

Smart woman.

With the same efficiency of motion, Seth pulled off the elastic harness of his shoulder holster and shrugged out of his black T-shirt. *He* could stand bare-chested out in the open, but as he heard the first of his security detail running across the gangplank above them, he insisted she cover herself.

This time she let him slip the neck hole over her head and hold the sleeves for her to slide her slender arms into. She barely gritted her teeth as he smoothed

the hem down along her flanks. But he swore out loud
at the welts and bruises already forming on her beautiful skin. He glanced over at the Indian still writhing
on his side, trying to find relief from his pain.

Unless Ace had a death wish, he'd stay down.

Seth gathered the bounty of Rebecca's hair in his
hand and gently pulled it from inside his shirt. "You
okay?"

She nodded.

He kissed her.

But the dazed look in her tawny eyes as he pulled
away demanded he kiss her again. He tunneled his
fingers into her hair and gently covered her mouth. This
time, her eyes darted to his. Good. He saw stronger focus.
More color. He palmed her neck and kissed her again just
because he needed to. He needed to feel her lips moving
beneath his, even for one short, stolen moment.

The footsteps were on the steps behind him now. He
moved his hand to the point of her shoulder. "How bad
are you hurt?"

Her eyes were clear now. "Just some bruises and
cuts." She held her palms up to the dim glare from the
Riverboat. "They're little things."

"Cripes. You're bleeding." A dozen nicks peppered
one palm. Darker slivers of wood marred her fingers.
Seth pulled a bandanna from his back pocket and tied
it around the cuts on her hand. "You're going in the ambulance with Mel."

"I'll be fine." She huddled inside his shirt as security
swarmed around them. Orders were issued. Calls were
made. She squeezed his hand with her good one and
whispered, "Thank you. I knew you were a good guy."

SETH BORROWED A CLEAN SHIRT after he saw Ace loaded into the back of a police wagon. Teddy Wolfe made a timely appearance, expressing shock at Ace's attack and conveying false assurances that no such violence had ever taken place on the casino grounds before. For once, Seth didn't care about the bull that flowed from his mouth. As long as he kept his distance from Melissa and Rebecca, he'd let him spin his little PR moment into a denial of any wrongdoing.

He made a call of his own to Cooper Bellamy while paramedics worked on Melissa and Rebecca, hovering close enough to hear things such as "He called her his wife, even though they're divorced.... Ace accused Melissa of betraying him...he indicated she'd been with another man. Like it's any of his business whether she sees someone or not—not that she would. She's a very private person, devoted to her son, not dating other men.... Yes, I believe he's hurt her before. I'd look up their divorce proceedings and see what grounds...wait..."

Seth grinned as she pointed out where the uniformed officer had misquoted her words in his notebook. God, she was a strong woman.

But that didn't make it any easier to stand by and watch her give her statement to the police while he was relegated to crowd control. Cops he knew—former friends who barely acknowledged him except to verify his permit to carry a gun and cast doubt on his ability to take down a guy twice his size with just his fists—arrived on the scene to cordon off the crime scene and conduct the interviews without him.

Like he told Coop last night in his truck, things

were about to bust wide open here at the Riverboat. He needed to watch every movement, absorb every detail. Who was nervous about Ace's arrest? Did any of them have more than a passing concern in the attack on Melissa?

Teddy and Kelleher were quick to get on their phones. Maybe it was nothing more mundane than a call to their insurance man to check for liability. Maybe it was something as important as initiating a cover-up so that Ace would take the fall for Melissa's assault and any other illegal activities at the casino that might be revealed by KCPD's overt investigation. Seth could track down the numbers called later. Shaw McDonough and Tom Sawyer were late to join the crowd of curious employees. And where the hell was Austin, anyway?

Whether he could flash his badge or probe for information under the table, he should be in the thick of things with the other cops, finding answers.

But when the ambulance left with Melissa and Rebecca inside, Seth left, too.

He'd given eight months of his life to this undercover assignment.

KCPD could grant him one night off.

"I'LL CALL you later," Seth promised, squeezing her hand. Dimmed for nighttime hours, the deserted third-floor hallway at K.C.'s Truman Medical Center was hardly the place for a romantic goodbye. "But I have to go take care of this."

Maybe it was just the players who couldn't make the romantic scene work.

Rebecca nodded and pushed him toward the

hospital's elevator doors. "I know. I hope Sarah's all right. I should have told you sooner. But with everything going on tonight, it slipped my mind."

"Understandable. There's no blame here." He ran his hand up and down her arm, instilling a warmth she couldn't quite hang on to. "I already called Coop. He's on his way over to her apartment to keep an eye on things. I just need to see for myself that she's gonna be okay."

"Teddy didn't hurt her, did he?"

Even with the golden stubble of his beard shading his neck and jaw, the dent of that line beside his mouth was evident. He was worried. "I don't think so. Maybe a little upset, though. Apparently, you were right about Dawn banging on the door. So it might just be embarrassment. But if Sarah found out about Austin's part in it…"

"Go." Melissa's black-haired little boy and golden-haired mother were asleep in the lobby chairs behind Rebecca, keeping a worried vigil over Melissa, still lying in a coma in one of the ICU rooms down the hall. Rebecca had no intention of leaving them until they had news of some improvement. "She's family. You need to take care of her."

His hand moved to her cheek. "Someone needs to take care of you, too."

Though a part of her leaped at the gentle suggestion, Rebecca forced her lips into a reassuring smile. "Get real, Cartwright. I can take care of myself."

He didn't take the bait and argue with her. Instead, he tangled his fingers in the hair at her nape and drew her closer. "I know you can. I just feel like I should."

"You saved my life tonight. You shouldn't feel like you owe me anything."

"I'm still gonna call you."

"Okay. Fine."

An orderly walked by with a stack of towels. Rebecca would have moved aside, away from Seth, but he wouldn't let her. "I'll call."

"Just go."

Seth gave a soft tug, pulling her close enough that Rebecca had to put her hands on his chest to keep from bumping into him. He ducked his head and angled his face to hers. She felt his warm breath on her cheek, felt the intensity of that storm-green gaze deep inside her.

"I. Will. Call."

When he leaned in and kissed her, Rebecca curled her fingers around the strap of his leather holster and held on. Her lips softened beneath his, parted for his tongue to find hers. She drank in his warmth and his promise, and tried to believe this caring stemmed from something more than guilt or concern.

Just as she felt him shift to deepen the kiss, the elevator bell dinged behind him, announcing its arrival a few moments before the doors slid open. Seth pulled away with a reluctant sigh. "I have to go." He frowned when she didn't immediately respond. "Bec…"

"I know. You'll call." She turned him, patted his shoulder and sent him on his way.

When the doors had closed behind him, she wandered back to the lobby.

With her cell phone lost at the bottom of the Missouri River, Rebecca crossed to a payphone. She had business of her own to take care of. The splinters had been removed from her hands, the contusions on her body inspected, the open wounds cleaned, salved and bandaged with gauze and tape. Her muscles ached and she was tired to the bone, but her mind was spinning with too many questions to simply go back and doze beside Melissa's family.

She waited until the first rays of sunrise lit the horizon before placing the call to John Kincaid. She'd still be waking him, but at least she wouldn't create the automatic concern caused by a phone call in the middle of the night.

Surprisingly, her father's old friend on the police force was wide awake when he answered his cell on the second ring. "Chief Kincaid."

He sounded crisp, efficient. Were administrators on duty at this time of the morning?

"John?" The buzz of voices and noise in the background told her he was at precinct headquarters. Great. Now she felt guilty for disturbing him with a personal call. But she had to know. "It's Rebecca. I'm sorry to bother you at work."

"No. Don't apologize. Here, wait a minute." She heard a door close and the background noise quieted. "That's better. It's been a busy night. A lot of us had to report in early."

"What's going on?" Okay, so she was still a reporter. She had to ask.

And he had to evade her question, as usual. "Police business, dear. Once the dust settles and I get clearance to do so, I'll give you a call and share the scoop."

"Sure." The duty nurse slipped out of Melissa's

room down the hall. Judging by the unhurried pace of
the walk, there'd been no change in Mel's comatose
condition. Rebecca tucked her chin inside the neckline
of the oversize black T-shirt she wore, taking comfort
in the clean, masculine scent of the man who'd worn
it first. "That'd be great."

John's tone changed, growing more concerned at
her lack of enthusiasm. "Rebecca? Is everything all
right?"

Not everything. Her friend refused to wake up. Her
back ached like an old woman's. And once she'd told
Seth about Sarah's visit to Teddy's private rooms, he'd
fumed like the blessedly overprotective brother he was,
put in a call to somebody named Coop—and left.

He *should* go take care of his family. Rebecca
understood that kind of commitment. She'd sought
him out at the casino because she knew he *would* deal
with the situation and take care of his sister—and
maybe talk some sense and self-respect into his father's
head. She didn't need him here to hold her hand
through the wee hours of the morning. She didn't want
the kisses that scattered her thoughts or the bandied
words that challenged her intellect or the intense looks
that warmed her from head to toe and deep within.

He'd saved her life. Together, they'd saved Melissa's.

But that didn't mean she had a right to ask him to stay.

She was used to being alone, fending for herself,
staying strong.

She wasn't used to needing. Wanting.

She didn't know how to handle how much she
wished Seth was here with her right now.

"Rebecca?" John demanded a response. "What's wrong? Where are you calling from? I don't recognize the number."

"I'm at Truman Medical Center."

John swore. "Are you hurt? Was there an accident? I can get away—"

"No. It's all right. *I'm* all right." Physically, at any rate. She squeezed her eyes shut and prayed John Kincaid would give her a straight answer. "I need you to tell me that Seth Cartwright is still a cop. I know I haven't had a lot of good things to say about KCPD since Reuben's death, but please, please tell me that Seth is one of the good guys on your team."

"Why is it so important for you to know whether or not Cartwright is on the right side of the law?"

Rebecca opened her eyes. "Because I think I'm falling in love with him."

REBECCA REVIEWED the information in the printout on the desk beside her, then turned to the keyboard for another spurt of writing.

Ace Longbow has been an employee of Wolfe International for nearly four years. Even before the Commodore*'s purchase was completed and building permits for the Riverboat Casino were issued by the city, Mr. Longbow was working behind the scenes to expedite the successful launch of WI's latest endeavor. And just how did this known criminal "expedite" matters? Is it coincidence that initial resistance to allowing another casino to come to Kansas City disappeared after one influential member of the Economic Development Committee came into a mys-*

terious inheritance and changed his vote? Is it coincidence that the reporter investigating WI's alleged corruption and influence peddling wound up dead near the river, on the very spot where the new Riverboat now stands, thus alleviating the biggest threat to WI's success—the truth?

Rebecca's fingers slowed as she neared the end of her paragraph. She'd started this article dozens of times over the past few months. It still choked her up to write about Reuben's murder. But today there was more than grief and unanswered questions to slow her writing.

Melissa Teague had woken up at nine o'clock this morning. And while her doctor believed she would eventually make a full recovery, she was still too groggy to do much more than recognize her family. As much as Rebecca wanted to find out what *betrayal* she'd overheard Ace accuse Melissa of, she didn't have the heart to mention his name and frighten her all over again.

But it wasn't holes in her story or the concern for a friend that left Rebecca so unsettled this morning.

She glanced at the clock on her desk. Nearly 1:15 p.m. "Stop it," she chided herself. She picked up her father's notebook and thumbed through the pages she'd memorized long ago. Her gaze drifted again. 1:17 p.m. "You don't need him to keep his word to you."

But a soft, lonesome spot, hidden beneath the independent streak inside her, ached for Seth Cartwright to do just that. It was past lunchtime and Rebecca felt like a sentimental idiot for glancing over at the phone every few minutes. But, dammit, he'd said he'd call.

Just like KCPD had dragged their feet on Reuben's murder. Finding nothing but dead ends, they'd given up.

Seth had given up on her. She was a low priority for him. If he'd just stayed the jerk she'd first met a year ago. Okay, so truth be told, she'd given him plenty of reason to act like a jerk. And he'd only been interested in protecting his family. Like he was this morning. Only motivated to take care of the people who were important to him because he was a good man. With a deep sense of justice and... It was 1:23 p.m.

Rebecca closed her laptop, stuffed the report in a desk drawer and got up to fix herself a sandwich. Sitting and waiting had never been her best thing. She hadn't really expected Seth to call her—not after she'd caused him so much trouble on his investigation. And despite John Kincaid's hedging answer this morning, she was more sure than ever that Seth was working on an assignment at the casino. If Seth did call, it would only be as a courtesy. It wouldn't mean—

The bell at her front door buzzed. Thankful to interrupt that embarrassing mental freak-out, she went to the intercom and pressed the lobby button. "This is three-seventeen. Can I help you?"

"It's Seth. Feel like lettin' me in?"

Rebecca tried not to smile, tried not to feel that incredible sense of relief. She buzzed him in. "You're late, Cartwright."

Thirty seconds later, he announced himself at her door and Rebecca hurried to unlock it.

He'd changed into a fresh suit. Shaved. And had the nerve to stand outside her door in that cocky, hands-on-hips stance that spoke of strength, confidence—and made her crazy with wanting him.

"Better late than never, right?" His smirk wasn't quite a smile as she invited him in. "You alone?"

Painfully so. She shut the door behind him. "You said you'd call."

"I like face-to-face conversations better." He locked the door, hooked the chain, and pulled her into his arms. "So I can see into those gorgeous eyes when I'm talking to you."

He covered her mouth in a kiss that was all too brief and far too passionate. She leaned back against his arms as he rested his forehead against hers to give them both a chance to catch their breaths and have a proper conversation. "I heard Melissa's awake."

Rebecca nodded. "The doctor says she'll need some reconstructive surgery to repair her cheekbone. But with plenty of rest and no more stress, she should heal just fine. Her upset stomach? The doctor says she really does have an ulcer. Can you imagine—working day in and day out with the man who hits you? She's lucky she didn't have more than one ulcer." Rebecca's fingers twisted convulsively in the smooth light wool of Seth's lapels. "She's lucky...she's not dead."

"Hey." His green eyes lined up in front of hers, demanding she focus on the positive and not relive the negatives they couldn't change. "She's very much alive. And with Ace in jail, we're going to keep her that way." He smoothed a kinky tendril off her shoulder, tucked it behind her neck and cupped his hand there. "Thank you for helping me with Mel. Thank you for being there for her when I couldn't be. Thank you."

Rebecca's fingers stilled. "You care about her a lot, don't you?" In this newfound world of needing a man, of needing this particular man, she hadn't really considered that he might have feelings for someone else.

He gathered her unbandaged hand in his and held it so close to his heart that she could feel it beating beneath her palm. "I care about Mel the way I care about my sister."

"How is Sarah?"

His eyes clouded over and he released her. "She's fine. I guess. She was a little upset, from the sound of things." He scraped his hand across his jaw and paced across her living room. "Maybe it's more about being disillusioned with Austin than by anything that Teddy did. Though I can imagine that once he put the moves on her..." Seth squeezed his hand into a frustrated fist at his side and stared out the window as though the summer sunshine was an unfamiliar thing to him. "Apparently, Coop spent last night at her place. I guess she couldn't get ahold of me, so she turned to the closest thing she could get to a big brother."

"And that would be Coop?"

"Cooper Bellamy. He and I go way back."

"And he would be your...partner?"

Seth turned and looked her straight in the eye. He didn't avoid the question; he didn't make up another story to explain it away. "If I admit to being a cop, will you admit that you're at the Riverboat to find out who killed your father?"

Startled as she was by his words, she wasn't surprised that he knew. Seth was sharp enough to have known she had lied from the very beginning. He strolled back to the desk and picked up Reuben's picture. "I understand he was a good man. He tried to protect you. He tried to do what was right by you."

Two things Austin Cartwright had never done for his children.

The derision in his eyes warred with the longing in his voice. Rebecca joined him at the desk. She took the photograph from his hands and set it reverently on the desk. "Somewhere, deep in his heart, I know Austin loves you and Sarah."

"Don't defend him to me. He pimped his own daughter to Teddy Wolfe."

"You have to find a way to forgive him, Seth, so the hate doesn't eat you up inside. So it doesn't keep you from moving forward with your life."

His green eyes looked at her with doubt. "Just like you've forgiven KCPD for never solving your father's murder?"

Direct hit. "Seth, I—"

"At any rate, I just wanted to see for myself that you were all right after last night. I seem to be about a step behind when it comes to protecting the people I care about." He reached out to wrap one of her curls around the tip of his finger. "Will you be okay if I leave you now? Even though I'm a cop, is there anything you need from me?"

"Yes."

He turned and faced her square-on, waiting with determined expectation to grant her wish. Whatever it might be.

"Kiss me." Did that breathy voice really belong to her? Goose bumps pricked her arms as long-buried emotions tried to reveal themselves. "In the last forty-eight hours I've been spanked by a loser, mauled by a lech and attacked by a leviathan." She hugged herself, and wished Seth would do that for her. "I would like, very much, to feel a man's hands on me that..." His hands were already on her bare arms, rubbing away the chill. "Cares."

Seth nodded, pulled her closer, rested his forehead against hers. "I can do that." He pressed a kiss to the tip of her nose, then tilted his head to kiss her mouth. "I can do that."

He tunneled his fingers into her hair and tilted her head so that he could claim her mouth. And claim, he did—in the most patient, most thorough, most commanding seduction of her mouth she could imagine. There were tongues and teasing, gentle nips and leisurely explorations. Long before the proprietary rightness of his lips left hers to taste her neck and sup at the small bump of her collarbone, Rebecca had forgotten all about every other man.

There was only Seth. And Seth's kiss.

He nudged aside the collar of her blouse and traced the curve of her shoulder with his tongue. Every brush of his fingers aroused, every whisper of his tongue soothed.

"Tell me where I can touch you." He growled in a husky voice against her skin and even the very vibration of sound caressed her skin.

She slid her hands beneath his jacket and scooted it off his shoulders. "Anywhere. Everywhere."

His lips tickled as he laughed against the swell of her breast. "Where can I touch you so I don't hurt you?" He lifted his head to reclaim her mouth. Once. Twice. "I know you got banged up last night."

"Mostly my back." She chased his mouth when he leaned back to shrug out of his jacket. "And my left hand."

Though there didn't seem to be anything wrong with the nerves in that hand as it swept over the muscular hills and hollows of Seth's chest.

"So it doesn't hurt here?" His hands settled at either side of her waist.

"No." She tugged the shirt from his waistband and discovered the heat of bare skin matched the hard power of his body.

"How about here?" He closed his mouth over the pearled tip of one breast, wetting her, warming her though the ribbed cotton of her top.

"Seth." Heat flamed beneath the flick of his tongue and arced down to the possessive grasp of his hands, filling her with a heavy need.

Gentle and thorough suddenly seemed too tame. The push of strong wills and strong hearts was too hard to contain.

Rebecca tugged at the hem of his shirt, wanting it off him. Now. But a bandaged hand and a feverish need slowed the process and elicited a frustrated moan. "I can't…"

Seth obliged her by removing his holster and setting his gun safely on the desk, then stripping off his shirt and her own in concise, efficient moves that spoke little of romance but all about need.

Then she was in his arms again, standing mouth to mouth, chest to chest. He slid his hands down to her bottom, carefully avoiding her bruised back, and lifted her onto her toes, making her taller—making her hotter. "Does it hurt—?"

"No." She skimmed her fingers along his thick biceps, over his massive shoulders, into his short, spiky hair. She accepted each kiss and demanded more in return.

Seth pulled her into the masculine thrust behind his zipper and she moaned with the need to complete herself.

"Bed." From deep in his throat, the husky word was raw and potent. Was it a question or a demand? "Where is this leading, Bec?"

There was no other man's touch, with Seth's hands and mouth staking their claim on her. There was no other need than the yearning in her heart and the fire in her body to become one with him.

She wrapped her legs around his waist and pointed over his shoulder to the room behind him. "Bed."

Minutes later, they were naked in the middle of her four-poster's cool sheets. Through the haze of their passion, Seth never forgot her injuries, never forgot her needs.

He spread her legs and pulled her astride him, plunging his sheathed arousal deep inside her.

That bubble of lonely isolation deep inside her burst and floated away.

And when they were both spent, Rebecca collapsed on top of his sturdy, welcoming chest. He rolled them onto their sides and gathered her in the sheltering curve of his body.

"Sleep, Page." He whispered against her ear and kissed the back of her neck.

Not *Poochman*. Page.

This was real. Seth was real.

No lies. No mysteries. No hidden agendas to come between them.

For now, at least.

Rebecca snuggled closer. "I'm sleepin', Cartwright."

SETH HEARD his cell phone ringing far in the distance.

But half aroused and cocooned in a blanket of fiery warmth, he had no desire to open his eyes and welcome a new day. He blinked open one eye. Sunlight colored the sheers at the window orange and rose. Okay, so he didn't want to return to the same old day. The weight on top of his chest shifted and a waterfall of sable hair fell into his face and teased his nose with the exotic— erotic—scents of ginger and spice.

He opened both eyes wide, smiled and pressed a kiss to the crown of Rebecca's hair. He hadn't had sex in months. He still hadn't had sex. But he'd made love twice in one afternoon, alternating between gentle seduction and passionate demands in the true push-push of personalities he'd come to expect and admire with this woman.

"Excuse me, beautiful." Rebecca moaned a drowsy protest that got him to thinking about rolling her over and letting her have her way with him once again. But he'd only had two condoms with him. And, "My phone's ringing."

She scooted away and curled up with a pillow while Seth crawled out of bed. He'd learned firsthand that prickly, headstrong Rebecca Page liked to cuddle—

that was probably what the dozens of stuffed animals were for. But Seth smiled—he preferred volunteering for the job himself.

But the damn phone was ringing. He pulled on his shorts and slacks and padded out to the living room to take the call so she could grab a few extra winks of sleep.

He IDed the number, then answered. "Hey, Coop. What's up?"

Though Cooper had spent some time hand-holding with Sarah while Seth checked on Rebecca, apparently, his partner had found time to get into the precinct office. "Our time's running out, buddy. Ace Longbow is in the interview room with Chief Kincaid, talking his ass off. Says he went after his ex-wife because he thought she'd slept with Teddy Wolfe. Apparently, Wolfie has a thing for blondes. He heard a rumor at the office that one of the blondes in the casino was pregnant. So, of course, being the dim bulb that he is, he immediately thought his ex was the one who got knocked up."

"She has an ulcer, not a baby."

"Medical reports do confirm. But, hey, that's just the local gossip."

"You're calling me with useful information, right? If he can tell us who's behind the sleight-of-hand accounting I copied off Kelleher's laptop after the poker game—hell, Teddy, McDonough and Kelleher all had access to it—"

"That's not what Longbow's talkin' about."

"What then?"

"He says that during the assault, your girlfriend

identified herself as Rebecca Page. He knows she's a reporter. And he says he knows somethin' about her daddy's murder." A beat of stunned silence before Seth could kick his brain into gear. He had to get Rebecca out of the Riverboat, had to get her far away from Wolfe International and to a safe house. "I know how your mind's workin' right now, Seth. But what if we use her to help us?"

"No. No way."

"We can hold Longbow in isolation for maybe forty-eight hours. Would that give the two of you enough time to—"

"No. I won't put Rebecca in any more danger."

Seth could hear other detectives in the background discussing his case, discussing the best way to proceed to an arrest. But he wouldn't consider any options that involved putting a persistent reporter nose to nose with the men who'd murdered her father.

Yeah, Longbow was guilty. The bastard deserved to go away for a very long time. But there were other options to consider. "Grill him. Keep Longbow in the box and grill him. See if he gives you a name. Maybe in exchange for lesser charges."

"I thought he was Wolfe's enforcer."

"He is. But if we can solve Reuben Page's murder without Rebecca's help, that's how I want to do it. As much as I want to string Longbow up myself, we still have to uncover the mole in Wolfe's organization. There's a bigger fish out there. I intend to catch him."

"I'll have to run the new charges by the D.A." Coop's wise old insight couldn't be denied. "What if Rebecca doesn't listen to reason and heads back to the

Riverboat on her own? If her cover's exposed, then yours might be, too."

"I'll deal with her. Leave Rebecca to me. I'll keep her away."

A throat was cleared behind him. Seth hung up and turned to the bedroom door.

Wrapped up in a sheet, the sleep-rumpled siren looked adorable—and he would have taken her straight back to bed if she'd spoken any other words. But Rebecca's defiance was clear and precise. "Keep me away from what?"

Chapter Eleven

"I thought we agreed that you weren't coming back to the Riverboat again."

Rebecca hurried down the hallway on the lower deck, purposely keeping a couple of steps ahead—and, she hoped, out of reach—of Seth, who'd threatened to haul her off like a sack of potatoes if she risked her life by coming to the Riverboat again. "No. You said you didn't want me here. I didn't agree."

She swung the heavy set of bolt-cutters up into her grasp to cut the chain on the door that blocked her from the engine room. Maybe Seth wasn't lagging behind so much as hanging back to keep an eye out for anyone who might be following them.

"It's my fault that Ace found out who I am. If I'm still willing to come back and find the truth, then that's my problem, not yours or anyone else's. Damn." With her raw palm, it was hard to get the leverage she needed to break the chain.

"Here. Let me." He grabbed the bolt-cutters and scooted her aside, cutting through the heavy metal in one, two, three strikes. He caught the chain and carried it inside with him after he opened the hatch. "Make this fast," he ordered over his shoulder before sliding down the steep ladder that led to the engine room. "And if we hear anybody coming—anybody—this treasure hunt is over."

His hands on the backs of her thighs as he helped her down the ladder reminded her all too vividly of how they'd spent their afternoon together. Concerns and hard truths had given way to comfort and passion.

As soon as her feet hit the steel at the bottom, she twisted away from the heat that seared her with even that impersonal touch.

How dare he? How dare he give her such a beautiful afternoon? Share all that time loving and snuggling and talking—and still not understand what she needed most of all?

"The truth is in here, Cartwright." She pointed to the hatch door two feet above her head. "Dad's clues all point to this door. If he had any evidence with him that night, it's in here."

He eyed the circular lock skeptically. "And how do you expect to open that?"

"Boost me up."

There hadn't been time to find a stepladder, but Seth's shoulders would serve just as well. "Whatever. Let's just do it and be gone."

Ignoring the sturdy strength of his compact body—and pretending the precise way he controlled all those muscles to help—not hurt—her didn't tug at a tender place inside her—Rebecca climbed onto Seth's shoulders. He lifted her high enough to reach the turning mechanism easily enough, but time and moisture had rusted it into place. Even using the steel handle of the bolt-cutters as leverage, she couldn't get it to budge.

She cursed at her own inadequacies. "I am not going to come this close to finding the truth and lose it to a pile of rust."

"Get down." Seth was already kneeling again, and lifting her thighs to help her climb off his shoulders. "This is taking too long."

He was chasing her out already? "I'm not going to give up on—"

Seth jumped. He caught the rim of the wheel in his grip and hung there a few moments.

"What are you doing?"

"I saw this in a movie once." He pulled himself up one side of the wheel and jerked, using his weight as well as his strength to pry loose the gears inside. "If he could do it…" He pulled and jerked again. "Then so…" And again. "Can we."

His biceps swelled with a mighty pull-up, then he dropped his weight one more time. The wheel ground in protest. But paint chips popped off and the rusted gears began to turn.

"Down below," Seth warned. Rebecca backed away from the snowfall of paint and began to wonder if Mr. Intensity just might be getting into this whole treasure-hunt idea himself. But with every twist, the wheel turned more easily, and when it finally locked in the open position, Seth dropped to the floor and scooped her up onto his shoulders again. "Your turn."

Rebecca was almost jittery with the idea of finally finding the evidence her father had been killed for. After wiping her damp palms on her jeans, she pulled open the door and reached inside. It was damp and moldy and coated with unidentifiable yuck. "Move me a little to the right."

She touched something soft, crinkly. "Daddy?" She wrapped her fingers around the puffy square. "Put me down. Put me down."

She was already inspecting her prize when her feet touched the floor. Soggy. Stained. But intact. A padded envelope.

"Hell, Bec, open it already."

Seth's anticipation fueled her own. She slid her thumb beneath the sticky seal and pulled it open. Rebecca's knees would have buckled if Seth hadn't been there to hold onto.

"A disk." She pulled the clear plastic sheath from inside the envelope and read the initials marked on the label. "D.B. Dani Ballard." *DBD.* Her father's code. "Dani Ballard's disk. She was an intern with the Economic Development Committee back when Kansas City was deciding whether or not to allow Wolfe International to build its casino. I think she was feeding information on the proceedings—particularly the illegal ones—to my dad."

"And she was killed for her trouble."

Rebecca looked straight into those knowing green eyes. She shouldn't be surprised. "Yeah, yeah, so I've been checking into your story, too." He shrugged off his familiarity with her father's case. "My partner and I think the two murders are related."

"That makes three of us." Those were *not* tears welling up in her eyes. What could she possibly be feeling? Gratitude? Relief? Something more? Instead

of letting the tears fall, she brushed the flakes of paint
from Seth's shoulders, then wrapped her arms around
his neck and hugged him tight. "Thank you for believing in me. And my dad."

Seth's arms tightened around her briefly. Then he
pushed her away, picked up the bolt-cutters and
reached for her hand. "We can go now, right?"

Rebecca took his hand and nodded. "We can go."

"I LOVED YOU once." He stood at Danielle Ballard's
gravesite and placed a red rose over her name. As he
straightened, the evening breeze whispered through
the leaves of the trees around him, reminding him of
Danielle's soft golden hair and the way it would stir in
even the softest of breezes. "Hell, I still love you. I gave
you everything. Money. Information to take to your
committee. My heart. Everything. Yet you betrayed
me.

"No more, Blondie. No more."

His cell phone rang. Blame and mourning took a
temporary backseat to the expected call.

"Yes, Mr. Wolfe?"

Nice to wake him before breakfast on his side of the
pond for a change. "Well?"

"She's not pregnant. I took a blood sample and the
results came up negative. I already have a plan in place
to dispose of her."

"Good. And the other woman—the cocktail waitress?"

"She's a reporter."

Theodore Wolfe, Sr.'s laugh was pure condemnation. "You're joking. A reporter has been working at

the Riverboat? Right under Teddy's nose? I can't believe that boy comes from my sperm."

"There's more."

"Of course there is."

"The operation here is in jeopardy. New evidence has surfaced regarding the bribes we paid Councilman Morgan. It connects him directly to us. Apparently, the intern we eliminated three years ago made a copy of a disk with transaction records."

"I thought we disposed of that. That *you* disposed of that."

Don't you dare question my loyalty and service to you, old man.

He swallowed the taunt. "I thought it was lost when I killed Reuben Page. But as it turns out, it was only temporarily misplaced. I suggest pulling all funds, cutting the supply lines and letting the Riverboat go to bankruptcy."

"That will cost me millions."

"It'll keep Teddy out of jail." Not necessarily a bonus, to his way of thinking, but Daddy wouldn't want that. Very hard to get an heir from a jail cell.

"Fine. Make it happen." Theodore Wolfe sucked in the deep breath that always preceded his commands. "And Shaw? Get rid of the reporter."

"My pleasure."

Shaw hung up and walked down the hill to his car.

So Dawn Kingsley had claimed to be pregnant to get closer to Teddy. He could take out that bimbo without batting an eye.

But the reporter—Rebecca Page—was personal. Unfinished business. Longbow had had the right idea about scaring her off by striking at the things that mattered. But he hadn't taken the idea far enough. Shaw McDonough had something very explosive planned for her.

Three years ago, he'd killed her father to silence a story that could ruin the family business. He'd killed the woman he *loved* to protect that family business.

Rebecca Page—and maybe even her erstwhile lover, Cartwright—had to pay for his losses.

Somebody always had to pay.

REBECCA WATCHED the bustle of activity at the Fourth Precinct office, marvelling at how such chaos produced such hopeful results.

Things were breaking fast and furiously for the major case squad. The crime lab was pulling information from the corrupted disk her father had hidden in the bowels of the *Commodore.* Every computer and file from the Riverboat had been confiscated. Ace Longbow was naming names to keep the death penalty off the legal table at his trial. Through her notes and Seth's diligent efforts, they'd even been able to trace a money trail from drug trafficking through the casino and back across the ocean to Wolfe International's London office. Scotland Yard would take over the investigation from there.

They were shutting down Teddy Wolfe's American dream for good.

Impressive.

About as impressive as the compact, green-eyed bull of a detective who was welcomed home to his precinct with handshakes, apologies and even the occasional hug. Rebecca thought she might have a hard time reconciling Seth Cartwright with wearing a badge. But the brass and blue enamel star on his belt suited him.

Besides, John Kincaid had handpicked Seth for his assignment at the Riverboat. Handpicked by a man she respected, admired and loved like family. Good taste like that had to count for something.

And who was the quiet giant off in the corner, typing up a report at his desk? Tom Sawyer? No. Sawyer Kincaid, John's second eldest son. Grown and out of the house long before Rebecca had ever had a chance to meet him.

Along with his lanky partner, Cooper Bellamy, Seth hadn't been entirely alone on his undercover mission.

Truth be told, she hadn't been alone, either. Green eyes met her gold ones across the room as Seth sought her out on the fringe of the crowd. He'd never left her alone at all.

An hour later, she and green eyes were on the way to her apartment. Seth laced his fingers through hers. "You know, sweet as that Mustang is of yours, I'm kind of glad it has to go back into the shop for a paint job."

She squeezed his hand. "Why? Because there's more room in your front seat to make out?"

He laughed. "Good point. I was thinking I like chauffeuring you around town." He wrapped his arm around her waist. "And walking you up the stairs." He tucked her close to his side. "And doing all those old-fashioned, chauvinistic things that drive you nuts."

Rebecca turned at the lobby door, stopping him

with a hand at his chest. "They don't drive me nuts, Cartwright. You do."

She leaned in to kiss him and the world exploded around them. Literally.

Lights and color and billowing smoke flashed in her retinas. A concussive shock wave punched them into the brownstone wall. Seth threw his arms around her and pulled her to the sidewalk.

"Get down!"

"What's happening?" His gun was drawn. He was on his hands and knees above her. He was bleeding. "Seth?"

"Your car just went up in flames."

"What? My car?" She tried to roll to her feet. "I want to see."

"Forget it." Seth pulled her up the rest of the way and shoved her toward the lobby door. "Get up to your apartment. Now. I'm calling for backup."

She had scrapes and bruises, but that gash on his shoulder was deep and jagged and seeping blood. "You're hurt. Come with me."

He shook his head. "I need to assess the damage. See if there are any casualties. Control the crime scene."

"Casualties? Seth, I thought this was over. I thought KCPD had Wolfe International under control."

"You can write this as an addendum to your story. You know how a cornered animal will react."

"I don't care about the damn story, I care—" The car parked behind hers burst into flames with the heat from the initial blast.

"Go!"

Though she hated to leave Seth behind, alone and unguarded while she ran inside to safety, Rebecca tried to tell herself two things. First, Seth Cartwright was one of the finest cops KCPD had to offer. She believed that in her soul, just as she knew how deeply she loved him in her heart. And second, he hadn't said anything about not calling 911 herself. He hadn't said boo about not running upstairs to grab her camera to take pictures of the crime scene or pick up her notepad to jot details.

She couldn't be there with him, where the cars were burning. But she was damn sure going to do something to help.

Her call was made, backup assured. KCPD, KCFD and their paramedics were all on their way. Rebecca unlocked her door and turned straight for her desk and the camera.

But the moment she stepped inside, she knew she wasn't safe. The bomb on the street outside was over and done—a terrible, dangerous misstep. Nothing more than a distraction, perhaps—meant to drive her inside.

The real danger sat on her couch, cradling Dawn Kingsley's dead body. The aromatic scent of smoke on Teddy Wolfe's clothing filled the air. Dawn's lifeless eyes beneath the neat bullet hole in her forehead were a gruesome reminder of her father's dead body. And the gun aimed squarely at Rebecca's own midsection had deadly consequences in the hands of a man with wild, weeping eyes.

Recoiling against the door, Rebecca tried to make sense of all that was happening here. The direct approach had always worked best for her. "Teddy, what's going on?"

"Did you do this?" He stroked Dawn's blood-caked hair off her forehead with a surprisingly gentle caress. "Were you jealous? Dawn said she was pregnant with my child. I loved her." He had a damn odd way of showing it while he was alive. "Why did you kill her?"

"What?" Rebecca's gaze darted to the window. She could see the smoke and dust still rising in the air outside her window. But there was no way out. No way to shout for help, no place to run. "I didn't kill her. I don't own a gun."

"Maybe your boyfriend, then. He'd shoot to kill."

"That's crazy." She pointed to the window, actually walked over to it and opened it a few inches before Teddy came to his senses and waved her back to the middle of the room with his gun.

Has to be done. Rebecca pulled her father's precious ring from around her neck and tossed it over the railing of the fire escape. "Get away from the window," Teddy ordered.

"Somebody just tried to kill us outside. I've been down at the police station all morning. There's not a better alibi than that."

"But Shaw said… I found her body here." He lay Dawn out on the couch and stood. "She was right where he said it would be. He said you'd…"

"Shaw said I killed Dawn?" Anger and fear rallied her strength. If her mouth didn't get her killed first, it just might save her life. "Listen, Teddy. Here's the real deal. You may have a heart in you somewhere. And, yes, you may even have loved Dawn. But you are a bullying, back-stabbing, pompous jerk! I wouldn't want you if you were the last man on earth. I love Seth Cartwright. I have no reason to kill Dawn because I have no reason to want you."

Was that the rattle of the ladder at the base of the fire escape? *I could do it if I wanted to.* She prayed Seth had a sharp eye to spot the clue she'd dropped, and hadn't boasted when he'd made the claim that any man of any height could reach that ladder—could reach her—if he wanted to.

"Let's think this through rationally, Teddy."

Her former boss scratched at his temple with the barrel of the gun. "I don't want to think." Then he swung his hand out and leveled the gun at her. "I want satisfaction." Teddy had lost all his charm. He walked toward her. Stalked her. "I want you dead!"

"No, you don't." She backed away, but the desk trapped her. "You're angry at Shaw. *He* did this. He probably killed my father, too. The police were talking about how Wolfe International had someone in the States who was overseeing your father's interests here. Someone who would take care of the details you missed because you were…"

"What? Gambling? Whoring?" He swung the gun around to Dawn. "Falling in love?"

Footsteps pounded on the fire escape. Rebecca tried to move.

But Teddy spun around, ground the gun into her stomach and grabbed her by the throat. Rebecca's scream was stifled beneath his choking grasp. "My father expected me to fail. From the day he sent me to this godforsaken city, he expected me to fail!"

Rebecca's window shattered, and a compact bull of

a cop dove inside and rolled across the floor. "Get down, Bec! Now!"

Rebecca covered her head and dropped to the floor as Teddy turned his gun on Seth. Both men fired.

But there was never really any competition between the two men. Teddy's shot shattered what was left of Rebecca's window and Seth's shot pierced Teddy's heart.

The sting of gunpowder canceled out the scent of Teddy's cigars. The only sounds in the room was the thumping staccato of her heart and Seth's deep, steady breathing. "Son of a bitch. You don't do anything the easy way, do you Bec?"

Rebecca didn't bother getting to her feet. She didn't bother with platitudes or explanations or even ask if he was okay. She crawled straight over to Seth, took stock of the new cuts on his body and determined where his wounds hurt him the least. Then she wrapped her arms around him and hugged him tight.

"I love you, Seth Cartwright. I don't care how hard we push each other, I will always love you."

"I can handle that." He loosened her grip, but only long enough to holster his gun and get to a sitting position where he could pull her onto his lap and match her embrace. He raked his fingers into her hair and looked her straight in the eye. "Can you handle this? I love you, too."

He kissed her.

"Life will be crazy for us, won't it?"

She kissed him back.

"It sure won't be boring."

He kissed her again.

"Shaw McDonough's out there somewhere. He murdered Dawn. I think he killed my father, too."

"He's probably responsible for that explosion outside. The profile I put together on Wolfe International's mole in the U.S. indicates he'd be able to kill any number of ways. You'll have to go to a safe house until he's caught. He wants you dead, sweetheart."

"He'll want you dead, too."

They kissed each other deeply, pouring out their hearts and promises for the future.

But then Seth abruptly pulled away. He stroked her arms to apologize for the separation. "We can't be doin' this now."

She tried to smooth the shirt she'd wrinkled beneath her hands. "It's the dead bodies, isn't it?"

"And the backup. I can hear the sirens. Five'll get you ten that Cooper Bellamy is the first one on the scene."

Rebecca grew stern for a moment, and found the strength to stand. She helped her battered protector to his feet and led him out the door into the hall. Once the door was shut behind them, she backed him against the wall and flattened her palm at the center of his chest. "Don't you ever place a bet with me. Or for me. I know how much Austin hurt you. Don't ever do that."

Seth squeezed her hand against his chest, nodding his understanding. Expressing his thanks in the solid green splendor of his eyes. "There's only one gamble I will ever make in my life. And that's loving you." He kissed her hand and sealed the promise. Then he reached into his pocket and dropped a gold chain into her open palm.

"You dropped this." He curled her fingers around her father's ring and kissed her hand. "Reuben Page would be damn proud of you. I know I am."

* * * * *

Welcome to cowboy country...

Turn the page for a sneak preview of
TEXAS BABY
by
Kathleen O'Brien
An exciting new title from
Harlequin Superromance
for everyone who loves stories about the West.

Harlequin Superromance—
Where life and love weave together
in emotional and unforgettable ways.

CHAPTER ONE

CHASE TRANSFERRED his gaze to the road and identified a foreign spot on the horizon. A car. Almost half a mile away, where the straight, tree-lined drive met the public road. He could tell it was coming too fast, but judging the speed of a vehicle moving straight toward you was tricky.

It wasn't until it was about two hundred yards away that he realized the driver must be drunk...or crazy. Or both.

The guy was going maybe sixty. On a private drive, out here in ranch country, where kids or horses or tractors or stupid chickens might come darting out any minute, that was criminal. Chase straightened from his comfortable slouch and waved his hands.

"Slow down, you fool," he called out. He took the porch steps quickly and began walking fast down the driveway.

The car veered oddly, from one lane to another, then up onto the slight rise of the thick green spring grass. It just barely missed the fence.

"Slow down, damn it!"

He couldn't see the driver, and he didn't recognize

this automobile. It was small and old, and couldn't have cost much even when it was new. It was probably white, but now it needed either a wash or a new paint job or both.

"Damn it, what's wrong with you?"

At the last minute, he had to jump away, because the idiot behind the wheel clearly wasn't going to turn to avoid a collision. He couldn't believe it. The car kept coming, finally slowing a little, but it was too late.

Still going about thirty miles an hour, it slammed into the large, white-brick pillar that marked the front boundaries of the house. The pillar wasn't going to give an inch, so the car had to. The front end folded up like a paper fan.

It seemed to take forever for the car to settle, as if the trauma happened in slow motion, reverberating from the front to the back of the car in ripples of destruction. The front windshield suddenly seemed to ice over with lethal bits of glassy frost. Then the side windows exploded.

The front driver's door wrenched open, as if the car wanted to expel its contents. Metal buckled hideously. Small pieces, like hubcaps and mirrors, skipped and ricocheted insanely across the oyster-shell driveway.

Finally, everything was still. Into the silence, a plume of steam shot up like a geyser, smelling of rust and heat. Its snake-like hiss almost smothered the low, agonized moan of the driver.

Chase's anger had disappeared. He didn't feel anything but a dull sense of disbelief. Things like this didn't happen in real life. Not in his life. Maybe the sun had actually put him to sleep....

But he was already kneeling beside the car. The driver was a woman. The frosty glass-ice of the windshield was dotted with small flecks of blood. She must have hit it with her head, because just below her hairline a red liquid was seeping out. He touched it. He tried to wipe it away before it reached her eyebrow, though, of course that made no sense at all. Her eyes were shut.

Was she conscious? Did he dare move her? Her dress was covered in glass, and the metal of the car was sticking out lethally in all the wrong places.

Then he remembered, with an intense relief, that every good medical man in the county was here, just behind the house, drinking his champagne. He found his phone and paged Trent.

The woman moaned again.

Alive, then. Thank God for that.

He saw Trent coming toward him, starting out at a lope, but quickly switching to a full run.

"Get Dr. Marchant," Chase called. "Don't bother with 911."

Trent didn't take long to assess the situation. A fraction of a second, and he began pulling out his cell phone and running toward the house.

The yelling seemed to have roused the woman. She opened her eyes. They were blue and clouded with pain and confusion.

"Chase," she said.

His breath stalled. His head pulled back. "What?"

Her only answer was another moan, and he wondered if he had imagined the word. He reached around her and put his arm behind her shoulders. She was tiny. Probably petite by nature, but surely way too thin. He could feel her shoulder blades pushing against her skin, as fragile as the wishbone in a turkey.

She seemed to have passed out, so he put his other arm under her knees and lifted her out. He tried to avoid the jagged metal, but her skirt caught on a piece and the tearing sound seemed to wake her again.

"No," she said. "Please."

"I'm just trying to help," he said. "It's going to be all right."

She seemed profoundly distressed. She wriggled in his arms, and she was so weak, like a broken bird. It made him feel too big and brutish. And intrusive. As if touching her this way, his bare hands against the warm skin behind her knees, were somehow a transgression.

He wished he could be more delicate. But he smelled gasoline, and he knew it wasn't safe to leave her here.

Finally he heard the sound of voices, as guests began to run around the side of the house, alerted by Trent. Dr. Marchant was at the front, racing toward them as if he were forty instead of seventy. Susannah was right behind him, her green dress floating around her trim legs.

"Please," the woman in his arms murmured again. She looked at him, the expression in her blue eyes lost and bewildered. He wondered if she might be on drugs. Hitting her head on the windshield might account for this unfocused, glazed look, but it couldn't explain the crazy driving.

"Please, put me down. Susannah… The wedding…"

Chase's arms tightened instinctively, and he froze in his tracks. She whimpered, and he realized he might be hurting her. "Say that again?"

"The wedding. I have to stop it."

* * * * *

Be sure to look for TEXAS BABY,
available September 11, 2007,
as well as other fantastic Superromance titles
available in September.

HARLEQUIN *Super Romance*

Welcome to Cowboy Country...

TEXAS BABY

by Kathleen O'Brien

#1441

Chase Clayton doesn't know what to think.
A beautiful stranger has just crashed his
engagement party, demanding that he not
marry because she's pregnant with his baby.
But the kicker is—he's never seen her before.

Look for TEXAS BABY and other fantastic
Superromance titles on sale September 2007.

Available wherever books are sold.

HARLEQUIN *Super Romance*

**Where life and love weave together
in emotional and unforgettable ways.**

REQUEST YOUR FREE BOOKS!

2 FREE NOVELS PLUS 2 FREE GIFTS!

HARLEQUIN®

INTRIGUE®

Breathtaking Romantic Suspense

YES! Please send me 2 FREE Harlequin Intrigue® novels and my 2 FREE gifts. After receiving them, if I don't wish to receive any more books, I can return the shipping statement marked "cancel." If I don't cancel, I will receive 6 brand-new novels every month and be billed just $4.24 per book in the U.S., or $4.99 per book in Canada, plus 25¢ shipping and handling per book and applicable taxes, if any*. That's a savings of close to 15% off the cover price! I understand that accepting the 2 free books and gifts places me under no obligation to buy anything. I can always return a shipment and cancel at any time. Even if I never buy another book from Harlequin, the two free books and gifts are mine to keep forever.

182 HDN EEZ7   382 HDN EEZK

Name	(PLEASE PRINT)	
Address		Apt. #
City	State/Prov.	Zip/Postal Code

Signature (if under 18, a parent or guardian must sign)

Mail to the **Harlequin Reader Service®**:
IN U.S.A.: P.O. Box 1867, Buffalo, NY 14240-1867
IN CANADA: P.O. Box 609, Fort Erie, Ontario L2A 5X3

Not valid to current Harlequin Intrigue subscribers.

Want to try two free books from another line?
Call 1-800-873-8635 or visit www.morefreebooks.com.

* Terms and prices subject to change without notice. NY residents add applicable sales tax. Canadian residents will be charged applicable provincial taxes and GST. This offer is limited to one order per household. All orders subject to approval. Credit or debit balances in a customer's account(s) may be offset by any other outstanding balance owed by or to the customer. Please allow 4 to 6 weeks for delivery.

Your Privacy: Harlequin is committed to protecting your privacy. Our Privacy Policy is available online at www.eHarlequin.com or upon request from the Reader Service. From time to time we make our lists of customers available to reputable firms who may have a product or service of interest to you. If you would prefer we not share your name and address, please check here. ☐

HI07

® HARLEQUIN®

Mediterranean
NIGHTS™

*Experience glamour, elegance, mystery and revenge
aboard the high seas....*

Coming in September 2007...

BREAKING ALL
THE RULES

by

Marisa Carroll

Aboard the cruise ship *Alexandra's Dream* for
some R & R, sports journalist Lola Sandler is
surprised to spot pro-golfer Eric Lashman.
Years after walking away from the pro circuit
with no explanation to the public, Eric now
finds himself teaching aboard a cruise ship.

Lola smells a career-making exposé...
but their developing relationship may
force her to make a difficult choice.

Bailey DelMonico has finally
gotten her life on track, and is
passionate about her recent career
change. Nothing will stand in the way
of her becoming a doctor...that is,
until she's paired with the sharp-tongued
Dr. Ivan Munro.

Watch the sparks fly in

Doctor in
the House

by *USA TODAY* Bestselling Author

Marie Ferrarella

Available September 2007

Intrigued? Read more at
TheNextNovel.com

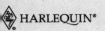

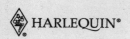

HARLEQUIN®

INTRIGUE®

COMING NEXT MONTH

#1011 RESTLESS WIND by Aimée Thurlo
Brotherhood of Warriors
Entrusted with the secrets of the Brotherhood of Warriors, Dana Seles must aid Ranger Blueeyes to prevent the secret Navajo order from extinction.

#1012 MEET ME AT MIDNIGHT by Jessica Andersen
Lights Out (Book 4 of 4)
On what was to be their first date, Secret Service agent Ty Jones and Gabriella Solano have only hours to rescue the kidnapped vice president.

#1013 INTIMATE DETAILS by Dana Marton
Mission: Redemption
On a mission to recover stolen WMDs, Gina Torno is caught by Cal Spencer. Do they have conflicting orders or is each just playing hard to get?

#1014 BLOWN AWAY by Elle James
After an American embassy bombing, T. J. Barton thought new love Sean McNeal died in the explosion. But when he reappears, T.J. and Sean must shadow the country's most powerful citizens in order to stop a high-class conspiracy.

#1015 NINE-MONTH PROTECTOR by Julie Miller
The Precinct: Vice Squad
After Sarah Cartwright witnesses a mob murder, it's up to Detective Cooper Bellamy to protect her—and her unborn child. But has he crossed the line in falling for his best friend's sister?

#1016 BODYGUARD CONFESSIONS by Donna Young
When the royal palace of Taer is attacked, Quamar Bazan Al Asadi begins a desperate race across the Sahara with presidential daughter Anna Cambridge and a five-month-old royal heir. Can they restore order before the rebels close in?

www.eHarlequin.com

HICNM0807